PATCHES ON THE SAME QUILT

by

BECKY MUSHKO

*One generation passeth away,
and another generation cometh:
but the earth abideth forever.*
—Ecclesiastes 1:4

*We may not all be cut from the same cloth,
But we're all patches on the same quilt.*
—Gillie Anne's sampler

Copyright ©2001 by Becky Mushko.
All rights reserved. No part of this book may be reproduced in any form without the permission of the author, except for brief excerpts used in reviews.

Single copies of *Patches on the Same Quilt* may be ordered from the author at (540) 576-3339 or e-mail at rmushko@infionline.net.

ISBN 0-9708129-2-2
Library of Congress Catalogue number TX5-423-426

Franklin Publishing
First printing, 2001
Second printing, 2003

Printed by Commonwealth Press
Radford, Virginia

Winner of the Smith Mountain Arts Council's first Creative Writing Contest for Novels and Collections of Short Stories

Patches on the Same Quilt is a series of related stories told by members of six generations of a rural Virginia family. A young boy's wish for a horse changes not only the direction of his own life but also the lives of his children, granddaughter, and great-granddaughter. As his grandmother, the quilt-maker Gillie Anne, says, "We might not be cut from the same cloth, but we're all patches on the same quilt." Each character's story adds a patch to the pattern of interconnected lives.

Author information: Becky Mushko, a retired public school teacher and current adjunct English instructor at Ferrum College, is a three-time winner of the Lonesome Pine Short Story Contest and a two-time winner of the Sherwood Anderson Short Story contest. One of her short stories was nominated for a Pushcart Prize by the editor of THEMA. Her humor column "Peevish Advice" appears monthly in *Blue Ridge Traditions*. Third generation owner of her family's Union Hall farm, she resides in Franklin County, Virginia with her husband and an assortment of dogs, cats, and horses.

Patches on the Same Quilt is her first novel.

Smith Mountain Arts Council

The Smith Mountain Arts Council (SMAC) is pleased to take an active role in supporting the publication of *Patches on the Same Quilt* as part of the organization's expanded outreach in the area of Literary Arts. *Patches*, a novel that includes a series of related stories about rural life in Virginia, was selected earlier this year as the winner in the Arts Council's first Creative Writing Contest for Novels and Collections of Short Stories. In addition to awarding Ms Mushko the $100 first prize, the Arts Council has contributed $2,000 toward the book's publication and will assist in promoting it. This adds a new dimension to the Smith Mountain Arts Council's efforts to foster a wide range of musical and artistic programs in the Smith Mountain Lake area.

The Arts Council is indebted to Jim Morrison, Chair of the Literary Arts Group, for organizing this new group under the "SMAC Umbrella" and for his dedication to enhancing the written word.

Donald E. Fink, President, Smith Mountain Arts Council

Becky Mushko is one of the most talented and prolific writers in southwest Virginia, perhaps in all of Virginia and even Appalachia. I've laughed at her "Peevish Advice" column in *Blue Ridge Traditions* Magazine, enjoyed her prize-winning short stories and essays, and been amused, stirred, and inspired by her poetry. With *Patches on the Same Quilt*, her first novel, Becky now shows that she is a contender in the heavy-weight class of novelists. *Patches* is a moving, beautifully-written book, with a real feel for rural Virginia over the last century and more.

Jim Morrison, First Vice President of the Virginia Writers Club and President of its Valley Writers Chapter; Chairman of Smith Mountain Arts Council Literary Arts Group

Besides SMAC, other financial contributors to the publication of this book include the Moorman Historical Lectureship, Blue Ridge Traditions (Peggy Ann Sloan Conklin), Bruce & Jan Cooke, Monroe & Kay Macpherson, and Jim & Edie Morrison.

Best wishes!
Becky Muchler

Foreword

Although it contains many truths, *Patches on the Same Quilt* is fiction. All major characters are not based on any actual person, living or dead. While a few very minor characters were based on actual people, they have been used fictitiously. Many places mentioned are real, but I have taken certain liberties with the geography of Franklin County, Virginia, so some places have been moved a few miles to accommodate the story. I have also tampered with history—though by only a few years—in regard to the time the railroad passed through Union Hall and Penhook. I thought it less of a sin to have the railroad run early than to have the Civil War run late.

That being said, there are many to whom I owe a huge debt of gratitude for their encouragement in my first attempt at writing a serious literary work:

Patches on the Same Quilt won the 2001 Smith Mountain Arts Council Fiction Contest. As part of the prize, SMAC generously chose my book to be the first that they helped publish. For the financial assistance, I am grateful.

I was fortunate to stable my mare at Hunting Hills Stable during its heyday in the late 1980's and beginning of the 1990's. The literary climate that prevailed in the barn provided a level of intellectual stimulation that I'm hard put to find nowadays.

Each year, Mountain Empire Community College in Big Stone Gap, Virginia, sponsors the Lonesome Pine Short Story Contest. In 1993, I entered the only story I had written in decades—"Forced Blossoms." Winning second place encouraged me to submit the story to a new Franklin County publication, *Blue Ridge Traditions*. Editor Peggy Ann Sloan Conklin used it in her third issue, and this gave me encouragement to try writing another story, "Last Wish," which Peggy again published. (Through the years, she's continued to use both fiction and non-fiction that I've submitted, plus she encouraged the writing and publication of this book.)

"Forced Blossoms," in a somewhat different form, became Chapter 7 of *Patches on the Same Quilt*. "Last Wish" was published twice before it became Chapter 1. Following its *Blue Ridge Traditions* debut, "Last Wish" was serialized in *4-Beat—The Journal of the North American Single-footing Horse Association*. When I read "Last Wish" to the sixth and seventh graders in my second period drama class at Ruffner Middle School in 1994, they thought I should expand it into a book. I decided to give it a try.

When Peggy Thornton, at Computer Wizards in Roanoke launched the publication, *Collage*, she asked me to write "something" and eventually I wrote a column, "Gone to the Dogs." From writing a series of columns, I realized I could also write a series of chapters.

Jerry Brooks edited this book and offered many valuable suggestions. A horse person/writer from Savoy, Texas, she had the seat next to my husband on a plane returning from Puerto Rico several years ago. As they conversed, he realized that she had a great deal in common with me, he got her e-mail address before she disembarked, and she and I met on the Internet.

Members of both Valley Writers and the Lake Writers listened to parts of this book and offered encouragement. Special thanks to Rodney Franklin who donated a ISBN number and to Jim Morrison, a true patron of the literary arts and my number one promoter, who opened the door to publication.

Mama started reading to me when I was a baby; later she took me to Western movies. That started my love of literature and love of horses. I grew up wishing for a horse just like Gene Autry's Champion. Eventually I got my wish.

My old dog Cracker lay at my feet as I typed the first half of the book. After Cracker's death, Jack the Dawg appeared at my farm in Penhook, and lay at my feet as I word-processed the last half. Every writer should have a good dog. Cracker was an excellent trail dog who loved following the horses; so is Jack. And neither ever found fault with my writing.

Finally, two equine ladies—my old racking mare G's Liberated Lady ("Cupcake") who brought me misery and joy in just about equal measure as I watched her grow from babyhood to old age, and Melody Sundance—the Tennessee walking horse who fulfilled my childhood dreams when I entered my second childhood—provided needed inspiration. Both mares have carried me over the same back roads of Penhook that appear in this book. It is to the easy-gaited horses like these, and to the people who want to preserve the natural gaits of easy-gaited horses, that this book is dedicated.

Becky Mushko
Novelty, Virginia

Prologue
JOHN ROBERT FORBES

EARLY MAY, 1865

*W*alk on, Sweet Molly. Can't be far now. I saw Smith Mountain shining green in the distance this dawn. How many hours ago was that? Five? Six?

We're on the right road for sure. Jus' gotta keep headin' west.

I confess I dozed a while and I thought you and me was back home and I was ridin' you to church way I used to do. Recollect? All them pretty girls who looked at us? And you rackin' just as smooth? Sure, you recollect.

Good thing you stayed on the road while I dozed. One of us gotta keep a look out.

Won't be long now. Before long, both of us'll heal up good as new. I'll make it up to you what you been through. You can have pastures to graze much as you want. Oats in your box every night. Won't never have to hear guns and cannon again. Maybe we'll raise us a colt or two. You like that? You much too fine a mare not to be bred. Gotta be a good stallion left somewhere.

Damn my arm hurts! Seems like the oozin' has started up again. That's what's attractin' all the flies.

How many days we been on the road, Sweet Molly? I forget. Was it day before yesterday we passed Lynchburg, or was it longer?

There was a bunch of us not more than a week ago. I recollect that much. All of 'em but us turned off one road or another. Everybody in a hurry to get home. That's all right.

Look. We're almost home. You see the mountain? It means we're almost home. Jus' keep headin' west.

I promised Mama I'd come back. You reckon she'll be surprised I kept that promise? Wonder what she's doin' now? Cookin' dinner, most likely.

Damn, it's hot! Sweat pourin' off me. Flies 'bout to eat us up. I gotta remember not to swear in front of Mama. She wouldn't like that.

You keep on the road, Sweet Molly, case I doze off again. Don't stray off the road. We'll be home by supper time.

Chapter 1
JOHN FORBES WEBSTER

LAST WISH

I got part of my name—John Forbes—from my uncle, Mama's older brother who died because of the War. I got the last part—Webster—from Daddy, who was in the War, too, but lived to tell about it. He tells that it's how he met Mama. Up to a year ago, I had always lived in Salem, Virginia, where my daddy taught classics at the college, and my mama gave piano lessons. Mostly, my life consisted of going to school and practicing the piano and reading and playing with my friends.

And wishing for a horse.

What I have always wished for most is a horse of my own, but Daddy has always said no—it'd be too much expense and I don't need one because I can walk anywhere in town I want to go. We've had conversations about it many times. They've always gone something like this:

"I wisht I had a horse," I'd say.

"You have one every summer," he'd say. "What about Old Molly?"

"She's old. And she's lame. It ain't the same."

"Don't say *ain't*," he'd say. "It's common."

"Uncle Henry says *ain't*. Why can't I have a horse?"

"Uncle Henry is not you. It costs far too much to stable a horse in town. Besides you can walk anywhere you want to go."

"I still wisht I had my own horse."

"If wishes were horses, beggars would ride."

"Then I'd have a horse," I'd say.

So, I've made do with Old Molly who belongs to my Grampa and Gramma Forbes who live on a farm in Penhook.

Old Molly is what they call a singlefooter. Daddy once told me about horses like her.

"In Medieval Europe," he said in the voice he uses to talk to his college classes, "the knights rode chargers into battle. However, these chargers were trotting horses, and, while they could carry the weight of a fully-armored knight, they were very uncomfortable to ride for long distances. Therefore, in order to arrive at the battleground untired and ready to fight, the knight led his great charger but rode a smaller, more comfortable horse—they called them 'amblers' then; and these amblers moved with a smooth gliding gait. We call their gait a 'singlefoot' or a 'rack' now. Hence, we call these horses singlefooters, or, less commonly, racking horses. However, in later times, as the roads in Europe improved, people began travelling by carriage and the trotting breeds came into general favor. Now Geoffrey Chaucer, in his 'Canterbury Tales,' mentions the ambling horse in the tale of the Wife of Bath—" and then Daddy rambled on for a bit about literature.

Old Molly isn't much of a horse. I can't imagine the likes of her being ridden by a knight. She's been lame ever since I've known her, so I can't really ride her, but I pet her and brush her and sit on her and make believe I'm riding. When I was little, it was much easier to make believe. Old Molly was in the War—that's how come she's lame. Her left hind foot twists to the outside and there's a dent in her left hip where she was shot by Yankees. She belonged to my Uncle John Forbes, who I'm named for. I never knew him because he died before I was born. Uncle John used to call her Sweet Molly, and he'd race her come Sunday on the road they call the race-track in Union Hall. Union Hall is up the road a piece from Penhook. He'd race clear to Bethel Church and pretty girls would cheer when he won. All that was before the War.

Uncle Henry Washington Forbes, who is not my real uncle on account of him being colored, says used to she could rack so smooth that you could carry a dipper of whiskey a full mile and not spill a drop. He told me Uncle John won a five dollar bet doing just that, but Gramma was fit to be tied for she didn't hold with whiskey—especially on Sundays. That was a long time ago—before the War. Old Molly was about four years old then, and frisky.

Every first of June, when Uncle Henry picks me up at the Penhook depot after I have ridden a train half a day to get there, I always ask him to tell me about Sweet Molly and Uncle John Forbes, and he always does. Uncle Henry tells it something like this:

"Well, chile, I recollect back then Jubal Early was gittin' up some men to go and fight the Yankees and yo' Uncle John was bound to go in spite a yo' gramma bein' set agin it. Mist' John 'uz a handsome devil and he sho' cut a proud figger asettin' up on Sweet Molly and her a prancin' like she goin' to the fair. He figger on only bein' gone a little bit—they'd whup them Yankees in no time an' be home by late summer. Yo' gramma, she beg him not to go, but he won' have none a it. She 'fraid he git killed, but he jus' laugh and say, 'Mamma, I made my mind up to die an' be buried right here on my own land. I reckon I'll be back.' An' yo' gramma—she so put out with him she won' speak to him an' she say to that mare a his, 'Sweet Molly,' she say, 'I know you got mo' sense than him, so I tell you to bring my boy back alive to me. That all I wish. You do that, you have a home here forever.' "

"And then he rode off on Sweet Molly—racking up a storm—while all of you stood in the road and waved, except Gramma who wouldn't look, and he was gone for four years," I added, "and then Sweet Molly brought him home again."

"That she did, chile. I recollect I'uz cuttin' hay up in the big field by the road when I hear a horse whinny. Won' many horses left round here. War took 'em. So I drop my scythe an' run to the road an' there laid Mist' John where he slip to the ground an' Sweet Molly jus' standin' over him, guardin' him like. He done wrote yo' gramma that he get wounded right befo' surrender, but that he'uz all right and would come home soon. We waited an' waited. This'uz in early May when Sweet Molly brought him back. One arm a his was bandaged up and blood oozed out. He 'uz might nigh burnt up with fever. Molly 'uz skinny as a rail and had a chunk outten her left hip, and one hoof kindly twisted sideways. She cain't rack no mo', that for certain. She musta walked the whole hunerd miles from Appomattox carryin' Mist' John, and him a'hangin' onto her mane long as he could. Lucky Sweet Molly remember the way. She born on this place, never know no other home before the War. Horses got good memories. Anyhow, Mist' John jus' as skinny as can be, so he won't hard for me to pick up and tote to the house. Sweet Molly follow along jus' like a dog. Yo' gramma saw her boy and she cry, 'Thank you Lawd for bringin' him home alive!' He 'uz alive, that 'bout all.

"He live the rest of the summer an' into early fall, mostly jus' settin' in the yard while Sweet Molly graze around him. He talk some about the War and the places he been and the things he seen, but he never say how he git wounded. Maybe he try to think it don' happen. Sweet Molly fill out some on the good grass, 'cept for the piece outten her hip. I keep her doctored up with pine tar and sulfur, and the skin growed back and it healed some. Her hoof stay twisted, but it look like it don' hurt her none. Yo' grampa, he want to put her down at first, but Mist' John won' hear of it. He say, 'She serve me well. She deserve better.' 'Course yo' gramma bound to keep her part a the bargain 'bout that mare always havin' a home.

"Later that summer, yo' mama come back from Richmond where she been helpin' in Chimborazo hospital, and afore long come the man who 'uz goin' to be yo' daddy. She nurse him at the hospital after he git wounded at Cold Harbor. He so grateful, he up an' ask her to marry him right then, but she tell him to come find her when the War over, an' he did. He come all the way here to find her. They marry in late August and leave on a weddin' trip to Maryland to visit his people.

"Come that fall, Mist' John die settin' right there in the yard watchin' old Molly graze, and sho' 'nuff he'uz buried on his own land. Well, it'uz still his daddy's land, but it woulda been his, jus' like it'll be yours some day. So he got his wish. His dying words were 'She served me well.' Since that day, that mare ain't done a lick of work—'cept when you come and fret her."

Patches on the Same Quilt

That is how Uncle Henry always tells it, year after year, ever since I can remember. Two summers ago, I was old enough to ask more questions.

"How old is Old Molly now, Uncle Henry?"

"Lessee—she 'bout four when the War come. Add more than four to that."

"That's at least eight—maybe nine. It's been thirteen years since surender. That's twenty or twenty-one."

"I reckon you right. She gittin' up there."

"She ever had a colt?"

"Nah, both yo' grampa and me is too old to fool with breakin' one."

"But you trained both Gen and Kate," I said, pointing to the mules pulling the wagon that always picked me up at the depot.

"Yo' grampa bought 'em full-growed an' green-broke. It won't like startin' from scratch. A young colt's a heap a work. Sorta like a youngin'."

"What if Old Molly had one?"

Uncle Henry laughed. "Well, I reckon yo' grampa have to let you have it jus' to get shut a it." He looked over and saw me smiling. "But don' you be holdin' yo' breath waitin'," he continued, "Molly a mite old to git started." Then he laughed some more.

"How does a mare, uh, get started?"

Uncle Henry was quiet for a minute, studying the reins in his hands. He shook his head and laughed again. "Didn't yo' daddy tell you 'bout such?"

I shook my head. I figured, in spite of all his book learning, my daddy just didn't know much about horses.

"Well," he said, "a mare got to go to a stallion. That a man-horse. He got somethin' to give her to git a colt started."

I wanted to ask more about the process, but decided I ought not. We rode for a bit in silence. Obviously, Uncle Henry wasn't about to volunteer any more information. I changed the subject.

"Uncle Henry, why did you stay and keep working for Grampa when the slaves were freed?"

"You sure askin' questions today, ain't you?"

"Didn't you hear about emancipation?" I was proud of myself for knowing what the big word meant. I worried that maybe Uncle Henry didn't know the word and I might've embarrassed him.

"Yep," he answered. "Yo' grampa call us to the house and read to us 'bout 'mancipation an' said we'uz free to go if we saw fit. Buck an' Tom, they left the nex' day. I 'cided I'd stay."

"Why?" I asked. "Why did you decide to stay?"

We came to the crossing at Owens Branch. Uncle Henry let the mules stop and drink. At first I thought he wasn't going to answer me. Finally, he did.

"Wellsir," he began, "when I'uz a slave, freedom seemed to me like a great thing. But when I finally got free an' got to studyin' on it, it didn't seem like all that much. I was gittin' along in years. Who gonna hire me? Where'm I gonna go? Who gonna tend my wife Reeva's grave an' her two little babies' graves? I don' know any other family or any other home but the one I got right here. I jus' couldn' leave my home. Yo' grampa, he a good man. He always do right by me. Even when he'uz my master, he work right 'long side a me many a time, an' I don' b'lieve he ever ask me to do no job he won't do hisself. His daddy befo' him own me—an' bought Reeva from the Nevilles when I tell him I like to marry her. An' he fix it so we had us a Christian weddin', too—not any a this jumpin' the broom.

"When freedom come, I tol' yo' grampa I don' care right much for it if it mean I got to give up my home and family. He said I'uz welcome to stay as long as I want to, and he give me my cabin an' the piece of ground around it. I still work for him to help him out, but I can go if I want to. I jus' never wanted to. I'm kindly like Mist' John, wantin' to die on my own land an' be buried up there on the hill with Reeva. This my home an' I'uz free to stay. Now, anythin' else you need to know?"

I shook my head no. He slapped the reins against the mules' rumps and we lurched forward.

We rode in silence for a few minutes. Then we rounded the bend and reached the house. Gramma hustled out and hugged me and said how big I'd grown. Grampa came out and got my luggage and said the same thing, just like in the past few summers when I'd come here while Daddy went off to study classical ruins and Mama went with him. When I was little, Mamma used to come stay with me. And just like in past summers, I went inside to change out of my good suit and eat Gramma's good dinner. Uncle Henry nodded to me and drove the mules down to the barn to unhitch.

After dinner, I set out through the wood lot to the shady pasture where Old Molly usually grazed. She looked up at me, then kept biting off clumps of grass and chewing. I studied her. She must have been pretty once—her coat was still a bright red, though when I got closer I could see she'd roaned out considerable about her flanks. From the right side she still looked fine, but when I walked around her there was a space on her hip big enough to put my hand in. There was a thin scar in it where no hair grew. That happened before I was born, I thought. Before I was even born, this horse was wounded in battle. I tried to picture the smoke and the sounds of battle, but somehow I couldn't. All I could hear was the buzz of flies and Molly's chewing and the far-off drone of cicadas, so I tried to imagine me sitting up on her racking up a storm and carrying a dipper of whiskey and not spilling a drop while pretty girls cheered. What did Uncle John do with the whiskey after he'd won the race? Did he drink it? Was that why Gramma got so mad? I studied on it while I picked tangles from Old Molly's tail.

On the farm, one day pretty much flowed into the next with a kind of sameness that I found agreeable. The passage of time was marked by whatever crop was being sown or cultivated or harvested. Haying came no sooner than I arrived in early June, and the sweet smell of it always hung in my nose long after the last load was pitched into the loft. I helped out as best I could with my town-boy muscles, mostly toting water to Grampa and Uncle Henry and some neighbors who helped. We were blessed with a week of hot, dry weather that year—just what you want for making good hay that would feed Old Molly and the mules and the cows when winter came and I was back in Salem going to school. We finished late of a Saturday—it was dusky dark and I was bone-tired. After a hasty supper, I climbed the steps to my room and fell asleep. I slept a deep, dreamless sleep, undisturbed until Gramma called out to me, "Wake up, John Forbes! It's first Sunday."

I put on my good suit and ate a big breakfast of eggs the dominecker chickens had laid yesterday, sweet milk fresh from Belle the cow and cooled in the spring house, bread from flour made from wheat I'd helped cradle the year before, applesauce from apples I'd picked from the big tree in the back yard and watched Gramma can last summer, and ham from the pigs that I'd had the job of feeding last year. I took pride in being somehow responsible for producing the food I ate, but I tried not to think too much about the pigs. Luckily, I was always gone when hog-killing time came. A few summers back, I'd named the pigs and played with the little ones. When I'd come back at Christmas and looked for them, Uncle Henry told me as gently as he could what happened to them. I peeked into the smokehouse and saw what was left of them hanging like ghosts in their white covers. I wouldn't eat ham or bacon for a long time after that, but I finally got over it.

When breakfast was finished, we went to the buggy that Uncle Henry had hitched Kate to. She looked a little flashier than Gen, so she got to be the Sunday buggy mule. Uncle Henry would use Gen to ride to his own church in Union Hall. We went to Bethel Church, over the same red clay road where Uncle John used to race his Sweet Molly. As Kate trotted along, I tried for a mile or so to picture Uncle John's ride in my mind, but couldn't. Kate's slow clip-clopping didn't help. Suddenly, just as if I were dreaming it, I heard behind us the clicka-clacka beat of a horse fast-racking over the hard road. I looked around just in time to see a man on a big red horse tip his hat to Gramma and pass us, then disappear into the trees around the bend. I caught a glimpse of four white feet and a long, high-held tail that swayed in rhythm with the horse's racking gait. It was the prettiest sight I believe I'd ever seen. Kate snorted her disapproval. The picture formed in my mind of just how Uncle John must have looked on Sweet Molly, of how a knight looked hurrying to battle.

"That's Colonel Pemberton. He's up from Danville and he's stayin' with the Nevilles for awhile," Gramma said. Then she began reciting how he was kin to who and on what side. She took pride in always knowing who everybody was kin to. I didn't pay real close attention. All I could think of was that big, red horse—the kind of horse I'd yearned and wished for.

I saw the horse again when we got to church. It was hitched to a tree on the far side of the clearing, next to the woods instead of close by with the other horses and mules.

"Why doesn't Colonel Pemberton tie up closer to the church?" I asked Grampa.

"That's a stud horse," Grampa answered.

I looked puzzled.

"You don't want a stallion tied close to mare," he explained. "It might cause a disturbance."

Gramma gave him a hard look. He didn't explain anymore and I thought it best not to ask. One word stuck in my mind—stallion.

I fidgeted all through the long sermon. I got a few hard looks myself from Gramma when she caught me looking past her, trying to get a glimpse of the stallion through the small windows of the church. As soon as the last amen was said and the congregation rose up to go outside where everyone would visit and exchange news with each other, I ran over to where the stallion was tied to get a closer look at him. He was the most beautiful thing I'd ever seen. His copper-red hair gleamed in the sun. He had a long mane that was mostly a darker red than his body, but it had a few white strands mixed in. A wide white blaze ran the length of his face, and high up on the blaze—above his left eye—was a spot of red the size of a silver dollar. I wanted so bad to touch him but dared not.

"You like my horse, son?" said a voice so close behind me I jumped. "His name is Soldier's Joy."

"I like him just fine," I gasped to the tall man with wiry gray hair and a gray moustache.

"Well then, maybe you'd like to ride him?" he offered, unhitching the red horse and swinging himself into the saddle as easily as if he'd been a young man. "Come on."

He reached his hand down to me. I grasped it, and he swung me up behind him.

11

"Come up, Joy," he clucked to the horse and off we went, slow at first, and then faster and faster, clicking along so smooth we hardly seemed to touch the ground. I kept my arms wrapped around the man's waist and felt the scratchy material of his suit coat on my cheek. I didn't dare risk falling off. The red road melted beneath us and the trees beside the road were a green blur. This must be the way angels glide, I thought to myself, and I must be in heaven. If I breathed, I don't remember.

Too soon the wonderful ride came to an end. We clip-clopped to a halt near my grandparents. I slid down, breathless and happy beyond words.

"Your manners," Gramma reminded me.

"Oh. Thank you, sir. It was a fine ride," I said, but my words seemed lacking, weren't enough after I'd said them, but I didn't know any words that would do justice to such a grand ride as that.

"You're right welcome," the man replied. "I do believe Soldier's Joy enjoyed it too. Didn't you, Joy?" The man reached forward and touched Joy's mane, and the horse nodded just as if he were saying yes.

Gramma took me by the arm and led me to the buggy, or else I would have stood there admiring that horse all day.

On the way home, Kate seemed even slower and more plodding than usual. Soldier's Joy, I kept thinking. Soldier's Joy. I wished I had a horse as fine as that.

I couldn't sleep that night for thinking of him. I tossed and turned and kicked the covers off. Finally, I got out of bed and crept downstairs, feeling my way in the dark, and went outside into the night. I looked up at the stars, so many stars I couldn't count them. I thought to myself that all my kinfolks before me had looked at these same stars—my parents who were far away now in some strange land, Uncle John away at the War, my grandparents, and their grandparents back when America fought England, and theirs back in England and Scotland, and theirs further back to the French ones who came to England in 1066, and the ones before them who came from Rome to conquer the British Isles, and all the way back to the beginning of time, to Noah standing on the deck of his ark when the sky finally cleared after forty days and forty nights, and—I reckon—back to Adam himself. Looking at the stars that way made me feel small, but in a way it made me feel big, too, and a part of things bigger than myself. I should have wished on the first star, I told myself, but I didn't know which one that was. Maybe wishing on all of them—all the stars that ever shone—was even better, so I tried that. "Wish I may, wish I might, on all the stars I see tonight...." Then, comforted, I crept back to bed and pulled the covers over me again.

The summer stretched out before me. Every day I awoke to the same thought—Soldier's Joy—and went after breakfast to curry Old Molly who was so far from being like him that it made me feel sorry for her being like she was, and that made me feel sorry for me for not knowing her when she was young and spirited. Maybe she felt bad, too, for she seemed to grow contrary, and she snapped her teeth and kicked out at me. She peed a lot, too, standing in a funny way, so I told Uncle Henry that I thought she must be sick.

"She ain't ailin', boy. She jus' horsin'. I thought she'uz too old for that by now. She be all right in a few days. You don' worry none."

Still, I worried about Old Molly. Early the next morning—way before breakfast, before the rooster crowed and Gramma got up—I slipped out to see about her. It was barely daylight and so foggy, the pasture seemed like a faraway dream. I couldn't find her at first, but then I heard her whinny at the far end of the field, and—farther away—I heard another horse nicker an answer. I ran, stumbling, over fog-hidden rocks and briars, to where I'd heard her call. I finally found her at the furthest corner, where Grampa's land joins the Nevilles' line. She had worked up a sweat and was pacing back and forth against the rail fence. One rail—the top one—had somehow fallen down. Old Molly tossed her head, stamped her front feet, raised her tail, and peed every so often.

"Molly!" I called, but she didn't even look my way. Then I heard hoofbeats and a snort from just the other side of the fence, and I knew it must be Soldier's Joy. He came toward the fence and she leaned over to meet him. They touched noses, then she squealed and stamped. He pranced back and forth along the fence, then galloped alongside it, whinnying.

If I had not seen what happened next, I'd not have believed it. Old Molly squealed again, circled round, and ran toward the fence. Just when I thought she'd crash into it, she gathered herself up and leaped over. She banged her twisted foot as she jumped, but this didn't slow her down a bit, and she galloped off into the fog. It was the first time—the only time—I ever saw her gallop. I lost sight of her, but I could hear the sound of two galloping horses fading into the distance. I realized I ought to do something to get her back, but what? I sat on the rail and cried a bit for, in my powerlessness, I didn't know what else to do.

It was way past time for breakfast now, and Grampa and Uncle Henry would already be busy priming the tobacco and wouldn't have time to help me. I got up and struggled with the second rail. After a while, I worked one end loose and dropped it down onto the fallen top rail. I stepped over and went to find Old Molly myself. The sun had started to burn off the fog and I could track her easy—Joy's hoof-prints were even and straight, but Molly's twisted foot made it look like one of her hooves was going in a different direction from the others. I followed them for a good ways. Finally, I heard a whistle far in the distance and then heard Joy nicker not far from me. I knew Colonel Pemberton was calling him up to feed him. I heard Joy's hoofbeats as he galloped to get his breakfast. I hoped Old Molly wouldn't go with him. I kept following her tracks.

Later, when the sun was full up and the fog all gone, I found her down in the swampy bottom by Polecat Creek. She'd been cut some by the briars and she was dripping sweat. She stood with her head down, breathing hard and patiently waiting. She didn't even look up at me. I noticed some welts on her neck, but other than those and the briar scratches, she looked all right. I didn't know how I would lead her home, for I had no rope. I tugged on her forelock, but she didn't want to follow me. All I could figure to do was take off my britches and run the legs around her neck so I'd have some way to lead her. I tugged hard on my britches legs and started walking forward. This time she followed, slowly, as I pulled her after me. The briars scratched my bare legs something fierce and the skeeters near about ate me up, but this time I didn't cry.

At last, with considerable prodding, I got her over the one remaining rail and back into her own pasture. I put my britches back on even though they were soaked with Old Molly's sweat and made my scratches sting. It wasn't until I'd worked both rails back into place and stood catching my breath that I wondered if Joy gave Old Molly whatever it was that started a colt. I thought maybe so, for they'd been together a good while, but I hadn't been able to see whatever they'd been doing.

I hurried back to the house, though I'd long since missed breakfast. The kitchen was empty—Gramma must be in her garden by now, getting vegetables for dinner—and a cloth covered the table to keep flies away. I pulled it back, grabbed a few cold biscuits, and went to the tobacco field. I felt as if I'd let everybody down for not putting in a full day's work. Luckily, no one asked where I'd been.

First thing every morning, for the rest of the summer, I ran straight to the pasture to see if Old Molly had gotten a colt, but each day there was none. At least Old Molly wasn't contrary anymore, but it was small consolation for my disappointment.

In early August, I accompanied Uncle Henry to town to get some things for Gramma and we happened to pass by the depot in time to see Colonel Pemberton load Soldier's Joy onto a boxcar for the trip back to Danville. Colonel Pemberton tipped his hat to me and smiled before the door closed and the train chugged off. As I watched the train pull away, I knew that Old Molly would not get another chance to get whatever it was she needed from Soldier's Joy.

The end of the summer came too quickly. Before long, I was the one climbing onto the train. I tipped my hat to my grandparents and Uncle Henry the way I'd seen Colonel Pemberton do, but I didn't smile. The train pulled away, puffing and chugging, and I went back to my regular life in Salem. Mama, who'd arrived home the week before, met me at the station and, after clucking about how I was growing like a weed, hustled me off to buy me new school clothes.

The first day back at school—at recess—Ned Whittaker bragged to anybody who would listen about his dog Nellie having puppies. He supplied a good deal of details, noting how Nellie and the Barlow hound from across the alley had got stuck together and two months later the puppies came. Like an expert, he described how at first the puppies were blind and almost helpless, and how Nellie suckled them. I listened eagerly to his explanation of one of life's mysteries. After school, I followed him home to see the puppies, who were just now old enough to clamber over me and chew my ears.

That night I asked Daddy for one of the puppies.

"Only a few months ago, you wanted a horse, and now it's a puppy!" he exclaimed. " What will be next? A baby elephant? John Forbes, we simply cannot deal with the maintenance of a menagerie." He saw the look on my face and softened somewhat. "Perhaps, when you're a bit older, we'll discuss the matter further. But, as for now, my answer must remain no."

I should have been disappointed, but my mind got busy thinking. Maybe Old Molly just needed more time. Maybe she'd have four babies like Nellie. Would they be all right, blind and helpless in the pasture? The nights were already getting chilly. I did some figuring—October first would be two months, or was it October fifth? I could hardly wait for my grandparents' monthly letter to arrive.

When at last it did come, I was beside myself waiting for Mama to read it aloud, as was her custom, to Daddy and me. This, of course, meant we must wait until after supper. I gobbled my food so fast Mama feared I would choke. When the dishes were cleared and Daddy's pipe had been lit, Mama carefully—slowly—opened the envelope, slid out the letter, and started to read. She read the family news, the neighbor news, and the crop news while I fidgeted with expectation. Finally, "Tell John Forbes that Old Molly"—I was on the edge of my seat—"is fine and misses him." I was crestfallen, bereft.

Through November and December, Old Molly continued to be fine and miss me. We—my parents and I—went to the farm for Christmas as was our custom, and Old Molly was indeed fine, though she didn't seem to have missed me. I searched the pasture, hoping frisky colts would appear from behind trees to play with me, but none came. Wishing for something didn't make it so. All the way home, I felt sorry for myself.

Last summer, my parents had a change in their usual plans. Instead of traveling for only two months, my father had a chance to teach and study abroad for a year. My mother was invited to accompany him. It was, he explained to us, too big an opportunity for him to pass up and meant an advancement in his career. My grandparents would of course keep me, not only for the summer, but for the whole school year as well. I could walk to Dillard's Hill School. Mama worried that my education might suffer, but I promised to study hard and practice on Gramma's piano—even though it had a few keys that sometimes stuck. Mama worried some more, but packed up my clothes—many more than usual—and saw me off.

Uncle Henry, as usual, was there at the depot with the wagon. After we exchanged pleasantries, we loaded my considerable amount of luggage, climbed into the wagon, and drove off. We rode awhile in silence. I didn't ask my usual questions, for I knew all the answers by heart.

"How's Old Molly?" I finally asked, not really caring but feeling I ought to say something to break the silence.

"She jus' fine. She gittin' fat, though. I reckon she needs you to worry her some," he said. "So you gonna be a full-time farm boy now?" He laughed and slapped the reins on the mules' rumps to move them on a little faster.

When I'd settled in and been fussed over and told how tall I had gotten and eaten the customary good dinner, I went to the pasture more from force of habit than from actual desire to see Old Molly. She had gotten fat! It seemed harder than ever for her to limp along. I couldn't help but feel sorry for her and soon fell back into my routine of visiting her after breakfast and currying her and sitting on her. My legs had gotten much longer than the previous summer, but they still stuck out sidewise from Old Molly's fat belly.

Once again, I quickly adjusted to the sameness of farm life. Then one morning in early July, when I made my customary morning visit to her pasture, I found Old Molly lying down and groaning. I ran for Uncle Henry who was chopping weeds in his garden. When I told him why I needed him, he dropped his hoe, grabbed a length of rope, and followed me.

"I reckon she colicky," he said as we went. "We need to git her up and make her walk."

I could move a lot faster than Uncle Henry, so I reached her first. She was wet with sweat, even though the morning was fairly cool. A grayish mass poked from her rear end.

"Hurry!" I cried. "Her insides is coming out!" It sickened me to look and I turned away. Uncle Henry quickened his pace.

"Lawd God in Heaven!" he said when he got there. It was the first time I'd heard him take the name of the Lord in vain. "She birthin' a colt!" he exclaimed.

He told me to hold her head, probably—now that I think about it—to keep me out of the way. He pulled his handkerchief out of his hip pocket and laid it nearby. He grabbed the nearest part of the gray thing and pinched it open. A nose with a white blaze poked through. Quickly he rolled up his shirt-sleeves and reached inside Old Molly. I was surprised to see how far in his arm would go. Old Molly groaned. After what seemed like an eternity, he pulled his arm out and there in his fist were two tiny hooves. He changed his grip to both hands and pulled so hard sweat popped out all over his face and neck. If things happened slow before, they happened fast now. Old Molly grunted again and pushed while Uncle Henry pulled, and suddenly a perfect little horse slid out, still connected to Old Molly by something like a slimy piece of rope. Uncle Henry picked up his handkerchief and wiped out the little horse's nostrils. It snorted, and Old Molly looked around and nickered softly.

I watched, frozen in place, at this miracle I was witnessing. I could hear the dinner bell ringing for us, far away as if in some other world. Uncle Henry stepped back and mopped the sweat from his face with his sleeve. He looked at me, waiting. For the longest time, neither one of us spoke. Finally I did.

"You said last year if Old Molly ever had a colt it'd be mine," I said in a whisper, in case this was a dream and I didn't want to wake myself.

"Reckon I did," he said, "But at that time I ain't actually studied on her ever havin' one. What yo' grampa goin' to say?"

Since I didn't know the answer to that, I didn't say anything. I just watched the colt as it lay there, breathing air, letting the sunshine dry its red coat. I could see blood pulsing in the rope that connected them. Uncle Henry reached down and pinched the rope closed. Molly rolled a little to try to get to her feet and the rope broke. A lot of nasty stuff dropped from her. She gave up trying to rise just then, and reached her head toward the colt and began licking it dry. She made soft, nickering sounds to it.

I stepped closer for a better look. The colt had a wide white blaze with a little spot just like Soldier's Joy. Its hair gleamed like a polished copper coin. Three legs were white almost to the knee. Only the left hind was dark, and for the tiniest fragment of a moment, I feared it was twisted like Old Molly's, but it was not. I thought the colt was the prettiest thing I'd ever seen. It struggled to its feet, then fell back down. I wanted to help it up, to cradle it in my arms and protect it now and forever, but Uncle Henry motioned me to stand back.

"Nah, boy. It got to git up on its own. Ever' time it try, it git stronger. Leave it alone."

It struggled for a while, then stood and walked in hesitant, wobbly little steps. All four legs worked fine. Old Molly was breathing hard and lay still.

"Giddap, move!" Uncle Henry ordered, and uncoiled the rope he'd brought and put it around her neck. He pulled until slowly she rose to her feet. She shook herself and nickered to her colt who was nosing around her flank.

"The colt got to drink the first milk she give to make it strong, else it die," Uncle Henry explained.

Then we stood in silence and watched as the colt found what it was looking for and pulled and drank and grew stronger. We didn't hear Grampa until he was right behind us. I didn't know yet how I would explain what happened.

"You didn't finish your chores or come to dinner. Your gramma was worried," he said. He stared at the miracle. Then, "John Forbes, what do you know of this? That colt is the image of Soldier's Joy!"

"The rail was down one day last summer. Old Molly got into the other field where Joy was," I began and then poured out the rest of the story, finishing with the plea, "It's mine, isn't it? Uncle Henry said if she ever had a colt, it'd be mine."

Uncle Henry lowered his eyes, not meeting Grampa's gaze.

"Maybe so, maybe not," said Grampa. "I believe you owe the colonel a stud fee for Soldier's Joy's service. If I'm not mistaken, he gets a right smart price."

"What's a stud fee?" I asked, and Grampa explained it to me. This was a problem I hadn't considered, hadn't even known to consider. I had almost no money to speak of.

"But the colonel didn't even know," I said. "Must we tell him?"

Grampa didn't answer but looked me in the face, hard. I knew what the answer had to be.

"Uncle Henry," said Grampa, "what part did you have in all this?"

"Nothin', suh," said Uncle Henry, " 'cept pullin' the colt outta its mama on account she too weak to push."

Grampa nodded. "Well," he said to Uncle Henry, "is it a mare-colt or a horse-colt?"

"Tell you the truth, I ain't looked yet," said Uncle Henry. He stepped in closer and knelt down beside the suckling baby. "It's a mare-colt," he said. "What you gonna call her, John Forbes?"

I looked at Grampa who pressed his lips together and said nothing. I thought of Soldier's Joy and how this little horse was almost his image, and how I felt the first time I saw him and rode him, and how I felt a few minutes ago watching the little horse takes its first steps and find the milk.

"Joyful," I said at last. "I'm naming her Joyful."

At the very moment I said her name, she stopped suckling, looked in my direction, and took a few steps toward me. I held out my hand and she sniffed it with her velvet nose. I ran my hand down her neck, feeling her fuzzy little mane, and across her back where someday I'd sit. I thought I would swell up and bust with happiness.

Old Molly then moved off slowly to graze, and her baby frisked beside her.

Patches on the Same Quilt

"She got a natural rack," Uncle Henry noted. Grampa nodded in agreement, and I thought I saw him smile a little bit.

"We'd best get back to dinner," he said. "Your grandmother must be out of her mind with worry."

He started in the direction of the house and I followed, looking back every few steps at this wonderful thing that had happened. Joyful, I thought to myself, savoring the name, Joyful.

The next few weeks passed in a waking dream. Every free moment, I ran to Old Molly's pasture and stared at Joyful. My eyes couldn't look at her hard enough.

One morning after breakfast, as I started toward the pasture, Grampa stopped me.

"Come go with me today," he told me. "We've got something that needs taking care of."

I followed him out to the wagon where the mules were already hitched. He answered the question before I asked it: "Colonel Pemberton is at the Neville's now. You need to settle up with him."

I worried the whole way. Would he take Joyful from me?

We finally pulled up to the Neville's house. Grampa whoaed the mules and hitched them to the post, walked across the yard to the porch, climbed the front porch steps, walked across the porch to the door, and knocked with the heavy brass door knocker. I followed behind him, dreading this the way I might dread having a tooth pulled. I could hear footsteps—like the footsteps of doom—treading across the wooden floor inside. Then Colonel Pemberton himself opened the door and showed us into the front room. Grampa told him why we'd come. Colonel Pemberton listened without saying a word, only nodding sometimes or fingering his moustache. I watched his face intently, hoping to see some favorable sign.

"So," Grampa concluded, "I believe John Forbes here owes you for Soldier's Joy's services."

An eternity passed before the colonel answered. "I usually get twenty-five dollars for Joy's fee, but this," he said, "seems to be a rather unusual arrangement. I believe I'd like to examine the filly before I decide on the exact amount. Would tomorrow be suitable for me to stop by?"

Grampa agreed, and they worked out a time. Then Grampa and I left.

I couldn't sleep a wink that night for worrying. I got out of bed and leaned out the window and looked up at the sky. I saw all the stars that had shone on me the previous summer. I'd wished before, and my wish had come true. Did you only get one wish in life, or did you get more? I wished again, as hard as I could, with all my heart and soul.

Early the next morning, Grampa sent me to bring Old Molly and Joyful from the pasture to the barn lot. Old Molly walked slowly, but Joyful ran ahead and then back, never straying far from her mama. She's the prettiest thing I ever saw, I thought.

When the three of us got to the barn lot, Colonel Pemberton was already there with Grampa. He studied Joyful, and ran his hands over her body and legs. She stamped impatiently, and when he released her, she racked off a bit with her tail held high.

"No doubt she's Joy's get," the colonel said. "She certainly has both his looks and his gait. I do believe she's the finest filly he's sired."

I don't know how my heart could both burst with pride and shrink with disappointment at the same time, but I felt like it did. I was so proud he liked her, but I knew if he liked her too much, I could never afford his price.

He looked me full in the face.

"Would you sell her to me?" he asked. "I'll pay you a fair price."

My heart sank. I couldn't let her go.

"No, sir," I replied, knowing Grampa wouldn't approve of what I was saying. "I just can't. You see, I waited so long for my own horse. Please, sir, tell me how much I owe you for the stud fee so we can work out how I'll pay it."

Well," he said fingering his moustache. I noticed that was what he did whenever he was considering something. "Well, I'll tell you what. If you agree to show her at the fair when she's a three-year-old and advertise, so to speak, the fact that Joy's her sire, I'll forgive your debt. But if you ever decide to sell her, I claim the right of first refusal. Are those terms acceptable to you?"

"Yes sir," I replied. "I agree to that, sir. Thank you, sir."

Relief poured over me like rain. I bade him good-by and led Old Molly and Joyful back to the pasture. Colonel Pemberton stood with Grampa and watched us go.

That summer—last summer—passed all too quickly. Joyful grew, as Mama might say, like a weed. I started school at Dillard's Hill and day-dreamed all day about my wonderful filly. Every day, I ran all the way home and raced through my chores so I could work with her.

Uncle Henry pieced together a little leather halter, and with his help I halter-broke her and worked her a little on the long line. I taught her to lead politely and to stop when I said whoa. Uncle Henry forgot he was too old to fool with training a horse. Together, we taught her to pose stretched out like show horses do, so she'd be ready for the fair. Uncle Henry led her around while I walked beside her with my arm across her back so she would get used to the feel of a person and not buck when she was first ridden. She learned fast—almost as fast as she grew.

Fall gave way to winter, and winter to spring. As Joyful grew bigger and stronger, Old Molly got weaker and thinner. She seemed only a shadow of herself. Walking was such a struggle for her that she spent most of her time just standing in one place. I carried hay to her and piled it up around her so she could eat without much effort. Uncle Henry had worried about weaning Joyful, but it was no problem since Old Molly's milk just dried up and Joyful quickly developed a taste for oats and corn.

I hoped the new spring grass would perk Old Molly up, but it didn't. It made Joyful frisky—she got in the habit of meeting me at the gate and, after she'd nuzzled my hand to see if I had some sugar for her, racing ahead of me to where Old Molly waited. That's how it was the first Saturday in April when I went to the pasture. I was not surprised to see Old Molly lying down in a sunny spot. This time, however, Joyful hung back instead of going to her mother. I knew then, as I approached, that Old Molly was dead. When I touched her, I could feel the warmth leaving her body.

It took Uncle Henry and me most of the morning to dig her grave. Even though Old Molly was little more than skin and bones, it was all the two of us could do to drag her over and push her body into the hole. I picked up my shovel, ready to cover her, and stopped to lean on it a minute to rest. Uncle Henry sat down on a rock and wiped his face with his handkerchief. I saw Joyful over in the next field. She grazed as if nothing had happened. I stood still and watched her.

Right then, I saw the way I wanted the rest of my life to be. Even though Daddy had his heart set on me being in a profession, I knew all I ever wanted to be was a farmer. I knew he wanted me to go to college. Maybe if I went off and studied agriculture in college, he would accept my choice. Maybe not. But for now, I wanted to stay right here on the farm and finish school at Dillard's Hill and not go back to Salem. In a few years, I would take over the farm from Grampa and work the land myself. In another few years, I would marry the first pretty girl that admired Joyful when I came racking into the churchyard, and we'd have children and raise colts from Joyful and put in crops. We'd grow old and die and be buried on our own land.

Uncle Henry stood up and mopped his face again. Was it sweat or tears he wiped away? I couldn't tell. I scooped up a shovelful of dirt and started covering Old Molly. When it was done, I patted the dirt down with the back of the shovel.

"Seems like we ought to say a few words over her," said Uncle Henry, who had been quiet all through the burying.

I nodded and thought for a minute.

"She served me well," I said.

Chapter 2
COLONEL PEMBERTON

MY KINGDOM FOR A HORSE

I have always admired the works of William Shakespeare. They were an amusement to me in my youth; they are a comfort to me in my age.

As the son of a well-to-do Danville land-owner who'd studied at Mr. Jefferson's University, I was naturally introduced to the classics at an early age. At one time, when just a lad, I even fancied myself an actor and would recite whole soliloquies to myself for naught but my own amusement. I learned by heart the entire "Oh, for a muse of fire" speech from Henry V and would declaim it loudly from the barn loft. I would whisper "To be or not to be" from the forked limbs of my favorite climbing tree when a melancholy mood struck me. I was known to bellow "Now is the winter of our discontent" from a windy hill-top. I always performed for whatever guests Mama was entertaining at the moment, and she entertained frequently. Little Ezra, precocious child that he was, was always in demand by visitors to the Pemberton household.

What is acceptable in the parlor when one is young would be disgraceful in public when one comes of age, however, so I was dissuaded from treading the boards and thus disgracing the family. My brothers and I were prepared early for the roles we were expected to play in life: Lindsey, the eldest brother, would serve his country in the military; Elias, the middle brother, would serve God by entering the clergy; and I, Ezra, the youngest brother, would serve the family by managing the family estate. My sister was merely expected to marry well.

It was expected that I would enroll at the University, the better to fit myself for gentlemanly pursuits, and so I did. I was always at the top of my class in English literature. I attended whatever plays toured in the vicinity and, of course, continued reading. I forswore my youthful declamations.

My life would have continued on its predictable course, and I would have played out my assigned part until the final curtain, had it not been for the War. The War changed everything. As did so many young men that spring when the word came of secession, I took leave of my classmates and hurried home to Danville where, after bidding my family farewell, I enlisted.

I am proud to report that I was a willing and brave soldier, though no more so than many other soldiers, and I quickly rose through the ranks. Late in 1864, I was promoted to the rank of Captain; I never was a Colonel. That was my brother Lindsay who fell at Gettysburg. After the War, those who knew us, called me "Colonel" in honor of him. I led a seemingly charmed life, so I thought. Though death was all around me—indeed, I had close comrades die in my arms—for most of the War, the worst I suffered in battles were bruises and scrapes.

One day, however, my luck took a turn for the worse. It was late in the War, although we didn't know how late at the time—March 30, 1865—at a place called Five Forks. We were still discouraged after Petersburg. Fitzhugh Lee was leading us; Pickett's forces were there, too. Pickett had been ordered to hold his position at all costs, and it cost him heavily. Sheridan's cavalry badly out-numbered us, and Sheridan, ever relentless, kept hammering away at us, trying to chip away our defenses.

That early morning, we were breakfasting on what little parched corn we had left. We thought—hoped, rather—there'd be no fighting, the rain being so heavy and we so worn-out and hungry and half-naked. We made a pitiful cavalry unit. Our horses were so thin they could barely carry us. My mount was what must have been, in better days, a plow horse. We made do with what we had. We had no choice.

Suddenly, the cry came, "Yankees! To horse!"

As we quickly saddled our horses, Sheridan's men crashed through our lines. Some of us didn't have time to mount.

Fighting was close—all rain and mud and blood and confusion. Through the rain and smoke, we could scarcely see who was friend and who foe. The world was a morass of sabre clash and pistol fire.

I was at least mounted, but it did me little good. A bullet nicked my boot-top and passed into my horse, killing him instantly. I had no time to dismount before he fell, my left leg pinned beneath him.

I had seen much action throughout the War, but that moment was the first time I had truly and completely known fear. Was I to die ignobly trapped under a horse in the mud? Some of Shakespeare's words formed themselves in my mind, the words of the evil King Richard III: "A horse! A horse! My kingdom for a horse!"

At that instant, I knew how King Richard must have felt—powerless and small and vulnerable. I thought those words over and over—nay, prayed them!—as I desperately tried to dislodge my leg from under the dead weight of the horse. While continually looking over first one shoulder and then the other, for the battle had gotten close, I finally achieved success. My leg was free! I drew my sword, ready to defend myself, though how it could be much use from the ground, I did not know. I only knew that I would not go willingly to my death.

In that instant I spied the red horse, darting first one way and then another. He looked young, not battlewise, as if he'd just been pulled out of pasture. His saddlecloth revealed he was a Yankee horse. When he was about ten yards from me, I whistled, the piercing kind of whistle I'd used to call the hounds when I was a boy. I don't know why at that moment I did it, but I saw the horse's ears prick up, as if he knew someone were calling him, and he rushed headlong in my direction, searching.

I reached out and caught his dragging reins as he came by, and he stopped, trembling. I grabbed the stirrup and used it to pull myself to my feet. This action could have taken no more than a few seconds, but at the time it seemed to take hours. All around us the battle raged, but we stood as if in the calm of the eye of a storm. I soothed the colt by stroking his mane with my hand, and his trembling lessened. He was a stallion, I noticed; no doubt there'd been no time to geld him before he was impressed into service. I mounted him—though he was a bit prancey, reined him around, and joined my troops in hasty retreat. Blood flowed from where the bullet had grazed my leg and mingled with the red of his coat.

"Catch yourself a Yankee, did you, Capt'n?" one of my men yelled to me.

Later, in the relative safety of camp, with my leg stanched and bandaged and the horse tied to the picket line, I examined my captive. His teeth told me my hunch was correct—he was no more than three. Despite his protruding ribs and hipbones, he had an air of dignity. His wide white blaze, broken by a single spot above his eye, and his four white stockings gave him a flamboyant appearance. He had the rangy but elegant look of certain Kentucky horses. No doubt he had fine breeding, but it was unlikely I'd ever know what it was. I untied him and walked him a little ways off from camp, where a bit of grass still grew, and let him graze.

As I, still limping, led the young stallion back to camp, a fiddler around one of the campfires struck up the lively tune, "Soldier's Joy."

"That's your new name, boy," I said to him. "Whoever you were as a Yankee, you're now Soldier's Joy, and you're a Confederate horse."

The idea then struck me that he had indeed brought me joy. Had he not appeared when I whistled, I'd most likely have died in the field. I have often marveled how one single moment can alter the course of an entire lifetime—indeed, of history—and so it was for me the moment Soldier's Joy entered my life.

I rode him through the rest of the War—what there was left of it. I hated putting a saddle onto his pitifully boney back, but I had no choice. He bore his hardships with dignity. After the War, when I rode him back home to Danville, my first priority was to turn him out in the over-grown pastures, and he started to fill out. His coat became glossy. Because of his handsome looks and easy gait, neighbors started to admire him, and several asked to breed their mares to him. I charged a modest fee, but the small income from standing Soldier's Joy at stud helped immeasurably in those trying times.

The following year, when his first crop of foals arrived and people saw what superior specimens they were, I had more requests for his services. Joy plowed my fields and carried me across them. He pulled the wagon that hauled my tobacco to market and my grain to the mill. Slowly, surely, I put my life and my land back in order. I could not have done it without him. How lucky I was to have a horse who saved both my life and my livelihood. So magnificent he is to me that I cannot help but using words from Shakespeare's play *Henry V* to describe him:

> "He's of the colour of the nutmeg and of the heat of the ginger. It is a beast for Perseus: he is pure air and fire; and the dull elements of earth and water never appear in him, but only in patient stillness while his rider mounts him: he is indeed a horse...."

When that boy—Sam Forbes' grandson—got his filly from Soldier's Joy, how could I begrudge him? While I would have gladly purchased the filly, so fine was she, the boy's eyes as well as his words told me she'd never be for sale. I could not take his money—indeed, I suspected he had none to spare—so I made an agreement with him that he could repay me by showing the filly when she was a three-year-old. I assumed that he, being but a boy, would forget the agreement, but I was surprised to receive a letter from him nearly three years later. He had every intention of honoring his contract.

"Sir," he wrote in a scrawling hand, "Joyful is three now and we are ready to show. How do I go about it, and where do I take her?"

I wrote instructions as to what was required of horse and rider, what the rider must wear and how the horse should be turned out, and made the necessary arrangements for him to transport her by boxcar to Danville. I procured an entry form for him and sent that and my instructions by return mail. I told him I'd personally meet the train.

I arrived at the station just as the train pulled in. The boy was the first to embark and he looked around as if not sure of where to go. I called to him and his apprehension vanished.

"Your grandfather didn't accompany you?" I asked, in hopes that I'd visit with Samuel.

"No sir," the boy replied, "he had to tend the farm. But he let Uncle Henry come along to help me."

"Well," I said, "Let's get your filly off the train and let her stretch her legs."

When the boy and the old colored man unloaded her, Joyful was a trifle skittish and snorted at every unfamiliar thing, but she was by no means unnerved by the strange experience. She pranced a bit when I tied her to the back of my buggy for the brief walk to the fairgrounds, but by the time we put her in the rented stall, she seemed to settle considerably. I offered the boy lodging at my home, but he declined

"I'll sleep in her stall," he said. "She's never been away from home before. Likely she'll be scared."

"We'll be all right, sir," assured Uncle Henry. "Miz Forbes done packed us a good dinner."

I left them at the horse barn and went home alone.

When I returned the next afternoon, I brought my little niece Dorethea, who was visiting from Richmond. Although her mother had no interest in horseflesh, Dorethea loved horses and, despite her mother's admonitions that things equine should be of no interest for a young lady, was eager to see a horse show. I had two fillies and a colt entered, so prior to the show Dorethea accompanied me into the barn where my horses were stabled. I did not see the boy and the old colored man nor the filly. No doubt, the boy had saddled up early and was riding about the grounds, the better to accustom his mount to the strange sights and noise of the fairgrounds. I conferred briefly with my groom and riders and, it being several classes before my horses were to enter the ring, retired to the grandstand with Dorethea to watch the show.

During our wait, Dorethea and I amused ourselves by trying to pick the winners in the preliminary classes. The child had a remarkably good eye for one so young and a girl at that.

Consistently she always picked as her favorite a horse that placed at least in the top five.

"Well, Dorethea," I told her after she'd picked a first place winner, "you're a born horsewoman, aren't you? Do you ride?"

"Oh, no, Uncle Ezra, Mama won't hear of it," she said. She looked downcast, then added, "But I would so love to learn. Will you teach me?"

"I don't want to go against your mother's wishes," I told her, "but we shall see." Perhaps I could find some way to convince my over-protective sister that riding would be a desirable activity for a lonely child.

Then the three-year-old mare class was called, and my attention turned to my own two fillies. One of them—Maiden's Blush—jigged a bit as she came through the gate and shied as she took the first turn, but the other—Tempest—looked splendid.

"See there," I told Dorethea as I pointed out my filly. "There's the winner. Remember you saw Tempest in the barn?"

"I'm sorry, Uncle Ezra," she said solemnly, "but I must disagree. There's the winner. I'll bet you."

She pointed to Joyful, who glided so smoothly into the ring that she seemed to float in the air. Her red coat gleamed in the afternoon sun. The boy must have spent all morning brushing her. Words from Shakespeare's poem "Venus and Adonis" tumbled through my mnd, and I almost spoke them aloud:

"So did this horse excel a common one
In shape, in courage, colour, pace and bone.
Round-hoof'd, short-jointed, fetlocks shag and long,
Broad breast, full eye, small head and nostril wide,
High crest, short ears, straight legs and passing strong,
Thin mane, thick tail, broad buttock, tender hide:
Look, what a horse should have he did not lack,
Save a proud rider on so proud a back."

But this horse had a proud rider. The boy rode like a prince, and if he were nervous, he didn't show it. He rode loose and easy, as if he were circling a hayfield instead of a show ring.

Only the serious set to his jaw belied that this was not a pleasure ride.

The class was large—over thirty mares—and consequently so lengthy, it seemed interminable, the judge being unable to select a winner without a proper demonstration. I tried to keep my eyes on Tempest, Maiden's Blush having broken gait early, but occasionally my gaze strayed to Joyful. Both horses gave flawless performances. Had Shakespeare been viewing the class, he might have observed that "the earth sang" when the two fillies touched it. Twice the judge called for the horses to line up while he ordered a few worked on the rail. Both Tempest and Joyful were selected each time. Finally the judge dismissed all but ten entries and those he requested to work again. I tried to observe each and every one, and eventually was able to pick out subtle flaws—this one winged a trifle, that one was a bit short-strided, another slipped into a pace as it grew tired—but both Joyful and Tempest remained flawless, one so like the other that I wished the boy would sell me Joyful that I might have a matched set.

The class seemed to go on forever. I inquired of Dorethea if she might be ready to change her mind, but she steadfastly maintained that Joyful should win.

"Do you mean," I asked, "that you'd choose another horse over mine—over your own uncle's?"

"Your horse is quite good," she said tactfully, "but the other horse is better. I cannot help that, and that is how I make my choice. I'll not change my mind."

I could not help but be amused by her resolute stubborness. She was indeed a child after my own heart.

One by one, the other horses were called to the center of ring and lined up, until only Tempest and Joyful persevered. The two half-sisters must have made ten laps in front of the cheering crowd, until a collective gasp arose from the grandstand. It was over. Tempest had paced a step, and both crowd and judge noticed. Joyful received the blue.

"See, I told you!" squealed Dorethea, giving way to child-like glee. "I have won the bet. Now, Uncle Ezra, you must teach me to ride!"

"I don't recall making a specific bet," I told her. "We only made a general bet."

"Nevertheless," she said, "as a gentleman, you must honor your bargain. We shan't tell Mama a word about it."

The child had me there. Now it was a matter of honor.

"Very well," I agreed. "Now let us see to my horses."

Back in the barn, both grooms and riders apologized profusely, but I assured them that through no fault of theirs, the better horse had won.

"Even a child could see that," I added, winking at Dorethea.

My duties to my stablemen having concluded, I went to congratulate the winner. A crowd of horsemen surrounded him, and he was so busy attending to cooling his mount that it took a moment for him to notice me.

Handing the reins to the old man, he broke from the group of admirers and approached me.

"Well, sir," he said, "I did as we agreed. I'm sorry I had to defeat your horse in order to fulfill the agreement."

"Enough said," I told him. "You won fairly, and you have no reason to apologize for a job well done. However, I don't suppose you'd be interested in selling the filly? Or perhaps you'd consider a trade for something from my stable?"

The young man shook his head. "Joyful will always be my horse, sir. She'll never be for sale to anybody at any price. If I were Shakespeare," he added with a smile, "I might say that 'I will not change my horse with any that treads but on four pasterns.'"

Had I been he, those are the very words I'd have used.

Becky Mushko

Chapter 3
GILLIE ANNE FORBES

SOMETIMES YOU GOTTA UP AN' GO

"Well, if that gran'son o' mine don't marry that red-headed gal, my name is not Gillie Anne Forbes," I said to myself first time I saw Colonel Pemberton's niece walk through the doorway at Bethel Church.

Well, I know who I am. I'se right. I'se nearly always right with my notions on account I never come to no conclusion afore I'se pieced together the evidence. I'se good at piecin', too. Nothing I like better'n to fool with piecin' some patches together 'n make a quilt. I'se made some mighty purty quilts in my time, I tell you, an' I aim to make a heap more, God willin'.

After my gran'son John Forbes—only grandchile I'se got in the world, he'uz named for my boy John who died of a wound he got in the War—after he up an' went off to college in Blacksburg to study farmin'—Can you imagine? Studyin' farmin'! "Agriculture" they call it—he come right back here an' set up to farmin'. 'Course that'uz his right. This farm belongs to him whenever he wants it. He's been a big help to Samuel—that's my husband, Samuel is. Samuel's gittin' too old to do much anymore, though he'd never admit to it. Lord knows he tries to do. What he'd a done without Uncle Henry an' John Forbes to help him, I don't know. 'Course Uncle Henry is a old man hisself. No tellin' how long he'll be able to work.

Now, as good a farmer as John Forbes is gittin' to be, he ain't goin' to be able to do it all hisself. A man cain't look after a farm an' hisself, too. A man needs a good wife if he's gonna amount to anything. That's a fact.

Now, I commenced to studyin' on it, an' I reckoned they won't no good reason for him to git married as long as Samuel an' me was still here. I'se cookin' an' cleanin' an' cannin' an' washin' an' all—which o'course I ain't complainin' about doin'—but still an' all, he ought to have a wife do it for him.

My daughter Julia done bought herself a house in Rocky Mount not long after her husband Charles died while they was off in some foreign country or other. It'uz his heart. Don't you know, he won't never buried proper, though Julia knowed there'd be a place for him right up here on the hill amongst all our people. Buried at sea was what he was. Buried at sea! Did you ever hear tell of such? Dumped off'n a boat is more like it. But it ain't my place to say nothin' about it. What's done is done.

Anyway, Julia's been widdowed for several years now, an' here lately she's been after me time an' agin to come live with her. Me an' Samuel both. She's right well off—Charles left her a good bit of money, an' she gives piano lessons to some of the town chaps. An' she's got plenty room, so we won't git under each other's feet. Me an' Samuel ain't gittin' no younger.

I tell you, the more she asks, the better this movin' sounds. I been on this farm nigh about all my life—I'se married at sixteen, you know—an' I'se gittin' to where I want to see someplace else in the world. It's in the blood, don't you know. Samuel's people—his great grandparents—they just up an' left Scotland right after all that Culloden mess. Won't nothin' left for them to stay for, so they ended up in America. Well, his gran'parents come to Virginie, an' his parents, they come to this county. My people now—they's mostly from England—they come to Essex County in the 1680's—an' they gradually worked their way across the state 'til they got here. Essex County to Orange County to Bedford County where I'se born.

'Course I left Bedford when I married Samuel. A wife has gotta follow her man.

My Julia was the very same way—traipsin' all over creation after her Charles. When she was just a gal, she took a notion from when we boarded that school teacher that could play the piano so good that she wanted to up an' go off somewhere an' study piano-playin'. Well, we scraped up some money—which won't easy back then, times was so tight—an' sent her off to that Botetourt Springs Institute that the piano-playin' teacher told us about. Then the War come, an' my boy John went. Next thing you know, Julia decided to up an' go to the War, too.

She took off to Richmond with some gal she knowed from that school who was from there an' went to work in a hospital, of all places. I tried to tell her it won't fit nor decent work for a gal, but she up an' went anyway.

In the end, it all worked out for the best for Julia—that's where she met Charles that'uz to be her husban'—but it won't the best for John. He'uz shot in his left arm—March 2, 1865, it was—when the Yankees attacked General Early's men in the Valley an' beat 'em so bad. Lots of boys was took prisoner, but John got away. Even though he'uz hurt, General Early needed ev'ry man, so John went on to Richmond with him. He'd wrote me that he'uz wounded but didn't think it too bad. It won't so bad that he needed to be put in the hospital. Iff'n so, he might of seen Julia an' she'd took care of him.

Then it won't long til he come home, his arm near about eat up with infection, an' he died. I'd wished him home alive, y'see, an' I got my wish. You gotta be real careful what you wish for. Julia come on home not long after, an' then come the man she'd marry. After she'uz married, they up an' went just about ev'rywhere there was to go.

Now, John Forbes—my grandson—has been courtin' this red-headed gal from Richmond for better'n three weeks. I know what's comin'. I got a sampler that I made when I'se no older than that red-headed gal that I mean to give 'em for their engagement present. It's got little quilt pieces all around the edge—work so fine they ain't no way I could do the equal now, what with my eyes gitten' wore out. It'll have to do for now, but I mean to make 'em a nice quilt for a weddin' present.

I ain't said nothin' to John Forbes about it yet—he might not even know yet he's gittin' married, but I see it comin'. You piece together all them evenin's he's been courtin' her, an' before long you got a pattern looks mighty nigh' like a weddin'. That's the pattern I'se usin' for their quilt—the weddin' ring pattern. It don't look like much while you'uz workin' on it, but before you know it, you got all those rings lockin' onto one another. Same pattern repeats over an' over. It's a might purty thing, it is.

Now the way I see it, piecin' out a quilt is kinda like piecin' out your life. You got to plan out the pattern you want—see it in your mind first, see all them separate pieces an' how they'll fit together when you git 'em stitched.

You cain't be swayed neither by bright colors. Oh, they look fine an' fancy at first, but the colors'll run first time you wash 'em, an' then, where'll you be? An' you don't want piece goods too fine an' dainty—won't hold up to ev'ry day use. What good's a quilt you cain't use? It ain't worth much if all you can do is look at it. A good quilt's for usin'.

An' the stitches, they's part of it, too. You got to make your stitches small an' even. Too tight, they'll pucker. Too big an' loose, they'll catch on somethin' an' ravel out. Takes thought to make a quilt.

There I go agin, ramblin' on an' on. I'll set to work on that quilt an' finish it soon's we move to Rocky Mount. I'll sit on that porch o' Julia's, rockin' an' piecin' an' watchin' ev'rybody go by. Ought to be a heap o' things to see in town.

I'se tellin' Samuel just this mornin', I reckon it'uz time for us to up an' go.

Chapter 4
DORIE CABELL WEBSTER

THE FARMER TAKES A WIFE

Mama raised me as if I were her little hot-house flower. While her doting on me—her little Dorethea Victoria Cabell—has often been a source of aggravation for me, I suppose I can understand her position. She married my father rather late in her life, and even later in his. Though in her youth she had had a plethora of suitors, none had been quite good enough until Harrison Carter Cabell came along. He was worth waiting for, she had once told me. He was descended from several of Virginia's finest families, he was handsome and well-educated, and he owned enough property to support Mama in the style to which she became easily accustomed. I remember him mainly from portraits, he having died when I was quite small. He was tall and slender and had refined features. If he had been a horse, he would no doubt have been a Thoroughbred with an impeccable pedigree.

"He was always of a delicate constitution," Mama frequently explained, "and of course the hardships of serving in the War did not help his condition. He was, of course, indispensable to General Lee, so there was no question but that he would serve. After the War, the strain that had been placed on his heart took its toll and that is why he is no longer with us." At this point, she would dab at her eyes with the edge of the lace handkerchief she always kept at the ready in her sleeve.

When I was little, this seemed a reasonable explanation for why I had no father. I often wondered why I had no brothers or sisters, but Mama would not discuss the subject with me. I was "too delicate" to concern myself with such. Fortunately, my father had left us quite well-to-do in financial as well as social matters, so Mama never needed to concern herself with much of anything—except me and the variety of ladies' organizations of which she was a member. Consequently I enjoyed every advantage that maternal affection can bestow, as well as several disadvantages.

I was, unlike Mama, quite unimpressed with money or position. Having been indulged in some ways, I craved indulgence in others. For instance, I wanted to chose my own playmates, no matter if they were the washerwoman's daughters or the gardener's son, but Mama would have none of this mixing of classes, as she called it. I felt myself quite miserable and deprived, for those children enjoyed a freedom to run and play loudly and get as dirty as they pleased—all pleasures that were denied me. All the lovely frocks and pretty books and expensive toys that Mama bought me were naught if I couldn't share them with such amiable playmates. To distract me from such undesirable social liaisons, Mama embarked on a series of travels to relatives near and far. Most were quite tedious, but visits to my Uncle Ezra's plantation in Danville were among the most pleasant memories of my childhood.

It was from Uncle Ezra that I discovered my love of fine horses. Mama, of course was, as she often said, "quite scandalized," when I took to following Uncle Ezra to his stable and to accompanying him to horse shows and sales. Even when I was quite young, I prided myself, to Uncle Ezra's delight, to spotting many winners in the show-ring. Though I would have relished being able to boast of this talent to Mama, Uncle Ezra persuaded me to keep silent. In fact, one day while Mama was in attendance at some social event for ladies at the church, Uncle Ezra taught me how to ride. I caught on quickly. I had never before known such joy or such freedom. I made up my mind that riding was something I would pursue wholeheartedly. What Mama didn't know certainly wouldn't hurt her. I kept this secret from her for years.

Fortunately, when I became old enough for Mama to agree that I might go away to be educated, I persuaded her to consider a school for young ladies in Buena Vista where, I had surreptitiously learned, riding was a part of the curriculum. After corresponding at length with the headmistress and consulting with various relatives in Rockbridge County, Mama bundled me off into the great world. While I still led a sheltered existence, the school being rather strict, at least it was a different existence, and my family did have connections to several prominent families in nearby Lexington. Often, on weekends, I was a guest in one Lexington home or another, and I dutifully wrote Mama long letter detailing what a lovely time I had. I neglected, of course, to mention that fox-hunting in Rockbridge County was an essential part of my lovely time. Had she known that I, though elegantly attired in the riding habit Uncle Ezra sent me, hurtled over limestone walls at breakneck speeds, she indeed would have had reason to be "quite scandalized." Fortunately, I never had a serious accident, though I confess to being unseated several times. Explaining a broken limb to Mama would have been most awkward.

It was not long after the completion of my formal education, and before Mama and I were to embark on a grand tour of Europe, that we summered near the tiny town of Penhook in order to escape the stifling heat of Richmond. Mama and Uncle Ezra had arranged to stay with distant cousins, so this was to be an opportunity for me to acquaint myself with previously unfamiliar members of my family. I feared I would be most horribly bored with rural life, but two things happened to change my opinion—and, as it turned out, the course of my life.

The first thing was a wonderful gift from Uncle Ezra, who had arrived a few days before Mama and me. No sooner had we gotten settled, than he bade me cover my eyes and follow him. He led me outdoors and, I could tell from certain unmistakable odors, to the barn. There he ordered me not to move until he so directed. Then he went into the barn and apparently lead out the most beautiful mare I had ever seen, for when I opened my eyes, she was standing not two feet away from me. She was small and fine-boned, more a pony than a horse. Her finely chiseled head was topped by two dainty hooked ears, and a wide blaze ran the length of her face. She was almost the exact color of my hair, and she had four white stockings.

"This is Joy's last filly,' he said. "She's for you. Since she is barely more than a pony, I couldn't get a good price if I sold her, and I dread the thought of a child yanking her around roughly. I thought, perhaps, that you might like to have her."

I was quite speechless. What a fine present! Since I am also small and fine-boned, she would be much easier for me to mount than a big horse. She looked like a China Doll, and that is what I decided to name her. I would call her Dolly for short. I couldn't wait to ride her, so Uncle Ezra lifted me onto her back. I hoped the barn blocked the view from the house so Mama wouldn't see me riding both bareback and astride. I don't know which would scandalize her more.

"She's barely four," said Uncle Ezra, "and only green-broke. Do you think you can handle her?"

"Of course, I can!" I announced. "Oh, Uncle Ezra, how can I ever—"

He held up his hand to stop me from saying more. "The look on your face is thanks enough," he said. He handed me the lead rope and I rode her around and around the barn-lot. She had a lovely fast rack, quite easy to sit and quite stylish. Heads would surely turn when I rode her in public. I was glad I had secretly packed my riding habit.

"Now, what do you say we ride horseback to church tomorrow instead of taking the buggy?" Uncle Ezra proposed. "Oh, by the way, I took the liberty of buying you a new side-saddle. I'm sure your mother wouldn't dream of permitting you to ride astride."

I agreed that riding to church was an excellent idea. Suddenly, I knew this visit would be anything but boring.

The following morning, Mama was, of course, so scandalized that I would not be sedately sitting beside her in the buggy that she did not ask where the riding habit and sidesaddle came from, and I, of course, did not tell her. As I rode step for step with Uncle Ezra and his red gelding, I thought how wonderful it is to move through the world on a horse, how wonderful to feel the world swirl past and around me. I longed to gallop China Doll, but I dared not. Mama's face registered quite enough disapproval as it was.

As Uncle Ezra was helping me dismount, I could feel various people's eyes upon me, and I confess I was quite flattered at the attention. I did not know if they were merely curious or if their stares reflected admiration of Dolly or of me. As I contemplated which it might be, we tied the horses and started toward the church steps where we'd wait for Mama to arrive in the buggy with her cousins. When we were almost at the steps, I heard the unmistakable sound of another single-footing horse rapidly racking down the hard-packed road. Uncle Ezra took my arm and pointed me in the direction of the sound in time for me to see a horse quite similar to Dolly, only larger, approach. A handsome, dark-haired young man was astride that horse. Uncle Ezra noted that the mare was Dolly's half-sister and that I'd once cheered for her at a horse show in Danville years before.

Upon seeing Uncle Ezra, the young man dismounted, walked toward us, and tipped his hat. Before Uncle Ezra had properly reintroduced us, I blurted out, "That's the second prettiest mare I've ever seen."

The young man gaped at me and said nothing.

Uncle Ezra said, "John Forbes Webster, do you remember my niece, Dorie Cabell? You met briefly at the fair in Danville some years ago when Joyful was a three-year-old.

Mr. Webster then stammered some pleasantry or another. He made me feel quite uncomfortable the way he stared with those blue-gray eyes of his. I started to tell him about Dolly, but thought better of it, as Mama's buggy arrived and it was nearly time for services to begin.

The preacher droned on for what seemed like hours. I thought the service would never end.

After services, I was anxious to get back to Dolly. I hoped the flies hadn't irritated her. I longed to be on her back again, but Uncle Ezra insisted upon introducing his "favorite niece from Richmond" to several of his acquaintances, and it wouldn't do to cut them off. Fortunately, Mama picked up the conversation and kept it going, and I was able to slip away. By the time I returned to where the horses were tied, there was Mr. Webster, standing beside Dolly and admiring her.

"A fine filly," he said, looking so deeply into my eyes that I wasn't sure if he meant me or my horse. "She must be one of Soldier's Joy's," he continued. "She has that unmistakable look to her."

"Isn't she the most beautiful horse you ever saw?" I said.

"No," he replied, and laughed. His blue-gray eyes sparkled. "But she's possibly the second most beautiful. Is she fast? Does she have a smooth rack?"

I didn't know what to say. I wasn't used to boys—young men—talking horses. Most who spoke to me talked about frivolous things—or about me.

"I don't know how fast she is," I answered, "but her rack is impeccably smooth. Do you want to race?"

Whatever was I thinking? Mama would be quite scandalized.

"Yes," he said. "I believe I do."

He untied his mare. Even though Joyful must have been well along in years, she was still magnificent, a larger version of Dolly but without so much white, and with a small spot on her blaze.

"We'll start here," he said, drawing a line in the earth with his boot, and we'll rack to the chestnut tree yonder. Whoever breaks gait, loses." He pointed to the tree to make sure I knew. "Then, if you're willing, and if your filly hasn't broken gait, we'll gallop to Houseman's Ford to decide the winner. First one to the ford wins. Are you still willing?"

"Of course, I'm willing, Mr. Webster," I said.

He lifted me onto Dolly and then mounted his own mare. We brought the horses up to the line.

"You call it, Miss Cabell," he said.

I smiled sweetly at him in hopes of distracting him while I gathered my reins and shouted, "Go!"

Both horses racked for all they were worth. Dolly, being shorter, had to move so much faster to keep up, but she never once broke gait. Joyful surged ahead far enough for me to admire how Mr. Webster's dark hair curled about his neck. He was two lengths ahead when we reached the tree, but as we galloped, China Doll gained ground on the old mare.

Flying down the road on my beautiful horse, I felt euphoric. My hair blew loose behind me, and the wind whipped my face. Constraints melted away, and I became part of the horse itself, and—like Pegasus—we fairly flew. The two horses ran neck and neck. I urged Dolly on, but Mr. Webster did the same with his mare. Joyful and Dolly arrived at the ford at exactly the same moment. At first, I was too out of breath to speak.

What did I care if Mama was scandalized!

"Well," I said when I got my breath. "Your mare moves well for an aged horse."

"My mare," he said, "moves well for a horse of any age. I notice yours could not beat her."

"And yours," I said, not to be out-done, "could not beat mine either."

"I agree," he said. "We're well matched." Then he changed the subject—I think. "May I call on you while you're here visiting your relatives?" he asked.

He was certainly very forward, but I liked how his eyes sparkled. Were they blue or gray? Bluish-gray, I think.

"Yes," I said, "you certainly may."

Whatever would Mama say, I wondered. First I race, and then I encourage a beau. I also wondered what I might say to Mr. Webster next, but at that moment Uncle Ezra rode up and I was spared having to make conversation.

"Dorie!" said Uncle Ezra, "your mother is—"

"Yes I know," I said, "*quite scandalized*!"

He nodded and laughed. "Yes, she is that, but I'm certainly pleased with how you handle that filly. Did you win?" he asked.

"I believe I did," I said, and Mr. Webster and I both broke out in laughter.

The three of us rode back slowly to let the horses cool down. Mr. Webster spoke at length to Uncle Ezra, mostly about horses. He expressed his condolences at Soldier's Joy's demise, and invited Uncle Ezra to visit his farm that afternoon, for he wanted Uncle Ezra's opinion of a horse.

"Of course, Miss Cabell is welcome to join you," he said.

"I wouldn't miss it," I said. "Uncle Ezra can tell you I'm a very good judge of horse-flesh."

Mama was, as I had suspected, quite scandalized, but good breeding prohibited her from chastising me publicly. After dinner, when we were alone in our room, I felt the force of her sense of propriety.

"Whatever made you race like a... a...." she groped for words, "like a *commoner*? Have you no sense of your place? Whatever must people think? And going off with a boy you don't even know! Well, I'm—"

"Yes, I know," I said. "We're both *quite scandalized*. But I do know the boy—the young man. He is a friend of Uncle Ezra's, and I met him at the Danville Fair several years ago. In fact, he'll be calling on me while we're here—with Uncle Ezra's blessing, I believe."

"He's a farmer! *A farmer!*" Mama exclaimed. "Do you suppose I'll allow a farmer from this backwoods town to call on you?"

"But, Mama," I protested, "isn't Uncle Ezra a farmer, too?"

Mama was so exhausted by the events of the day, she lay down for a nap rather than try to reason with me. Her timing couldn't have been better, for it gave me the opportunity to slip away with Uncle Ezra for a ride to Mr. Webster's farm. Of course, Mama would later come to her senses and yield to her older brother's wishes.

On the way over, Uncle Ezra told me how Mr. Webster had decided when he was still a boy that he wanted nothing else in life but to raise horses and to farm, but to satisfy his parents' wishes he had gone away to college and then returned to manage the farm for his aging grandparents. Uncle Ezra spoke quite highly of him and pointed out how Mr. Webster was a respected farmer in the area, as well as an eligible young bachelor.

I couldn't help blushing, and hoped only that Uncle Ezra did not see.

When we arrived, Mrs. Forbes ushered us into her front room. The way she looked at me, I felt as if I might be a prize filly that she was considering. She was a most gracious hostess, offering us some light refreshment and asking Uncle Ezra about the rest of his family. While they chatted, I looked about the room. Mrs. Forbes' touch was everywhere. Two or three quilts with ornate patterns hung over the back of the settee and each wall was adorned with samplers she'd embroidered. She must have noticed me looking, for she said, "That's one of my favorites. I stitched it when I was about your age."

I rose and went closer for a look. "We may not be cut from the same cloth," it read, "but we're all patches on the same quilt." All around the border were tiny, tiny patches of different shades of silk. Each patch had a design quilted in stitches so intricate it was difficult to believe anyone could have had done it.

She watched me as I studied it. "I mean it to be what you call a heirloom," she said. "You know, one of them things handed down."

"Yes," I said, "it is a lovely heirloom."

She smiled. I believe she approved of me the way I approved of her work. At that moment, Mr. Webster came in and apologized for not being there to greet us himself.

"I was grooming a horse," he said. "I wanted it to look just right."

With that, he requested we follow him to the barn.

There in his barn were a dozen or so beautiful horses. With the exception of two bays, all were a variety of chestnut, with tones ranging from roan to deep copper red. As we walked through the barn, he talked of each horse as if it might be a child. He told me each horse's name and related information about each one that he thought might interest me. The magnificent stallion Jubilation occupied a large box stall at one end. Next to him was his mother Joyful. Then there were the other mares' stalls. All of them were either named a variant of "Joy"—"Wild Joy," "Ever Joyful," "Joyful Melody"—or else they bore the names of songs—"Ida Red" (who was indeed red), "Wildwood Flower," and the dark, lovely "Sonata." At the opposite end of the barn, in another box stall was Sonata's son, the two-year-old stallion "Night Music," a bright bay with the same wide white blaze the others bore.

I stood back and watched while Mr. Webster led him out for Uncle Ezra's inspection. The horse's coat gleamed as if he'd been polished. This one, I decided, must have been the one that Mr. Webster had been grooming when he lost track of time.

"He's too fine an animal to geld," Mr. Webster said to Uncle Ezra, "and since he's so closely related to most of my mares, I can't use him in my breeding program. I owe you a debt, sir, that I've never actually repaid. Surely the interest I owe you on Joy's stud fee so long ago must now equal this horse's worth. I realize not a horse living can replace Soldier's Joy, but I'd like you to have his great-grandson."

Uncle Ezra's lip trembled. He stepped forward and stroked the young horse's shoulder. "But you lived up to your part of the bargain," he said. "You showed Joyful at more shows than I ever expected you would."

"Please, sir," said Mr. Webster, "I'd like you to have him. I couldn't bear to sell him and not know what would become of him."

That was the moment I truly fell head over heels in love with Mr. Webster—with John Forbes.

He indeed came to call every night for the next three weeks. The first evening he came, Mama, who dared not leave him alone with me, played the piano so I could sing. Mama was quite proud of my singing voice and relished the opportunity to show me off—even to a gentleman she did not wish to impress.

"I hope Dorethea will always keep up her music," Mama said. "It is such a lovely and proper accomplishment for a young lady to demonstrate her accomplishment in music, don't you think, Mr. Webster?"

"I surely do," he replied.

"Do you play?" she inquired of him.

"Oh, just a bit," he said.

Mama moved from the piano stool. "Then I insist," she said, "that you should play for us."

He smiled. "If you insist," he said.

He ran his fingers over the keys and picked out a few hymns. From the corner of my eye, I saw Mama smiling as if she knew that she had shown him up. Then his fingers moved over the keys, and he began to play a quite complicated piece.

Mama stopped smiling and sputtered, "But that's Mozart! Wherever did you learn to play Mozart?"

It was Mr. Webster's turn to smile. "From my mother," he said. "One of the conditions that she allow me to become a farmer was that I should keep up my music. She thought the same as you, Mrs. Cabell, that music was a proper accomplishment for anyone. I had a dreadful time when I was away at college. At least, the boarding house where I lived had a piano in the parlor, but the other agriculture students ragged me mercilessly. 'What use is that kind of music for a farmer?' they'd say. 'Are you going to play to your cows?' Well, no matter. I kept my promise, and I do enjoy Mozart."

Mama was speechless, though only momentarily.

"Mr. Webster," she said, "you have my permission to call on Dorethea whenever you like."

I wanted to blurt out that he would call on me regardless, but thought better of it. Instead Mr. Webster—John Forbes—and I exchanged smiles.

The next Sunday after church, and after one of his grandmother's marvelous dinners, we rode across his land. He pointed out different fields and the different crops that he had planted. We rode up to his tenant's house, and he introduced me to Uncle Henry, an ancient but spry old man. Why did I feel that everyone I met at John Forbes' farm was appraising me?

"Yassuh, Mist' John," Uncle Henry said. "You always had you a good eye. I reckon I approve."

After we had bidden him good-by and ridden out of his hearing, I asked, "What, pray tell, Mr. Webster, was that all about?"

"Well," he said, "your mother had to approve of me. Uncle Henry had to approve of you. Now that it's done, there's nothing left but for me to ask you to marry me."

He dismounted and took hold of Dolly's bridle. "You will, won't you?"

I didn't want to appear to eager, but I couldn't help myself. "Yes," I said, looking down at him, "yes. I will."

49

He lifted me off my saddle, and there on a clear Sunday afternoon at the highest point of his top field, with Smith Mountain shining blue-green in the distance and a warm sun beaming down upon us, we kissed. It crossed my mind that he is like my knight in shining armor, but I dared not tell him so.

That evening, he officially asked Mama for my hand. She was nonplused. Eventually, she recovered her wits to give her reluctant consent.

"It shan't matter what I say," she said. "I expect you'll do as you please. You get this headstrong streak from your late father. Of course, you realize you're giving up the opportunity to travel through Europe and to live a grand life in Richmond. If being a farmer's wife is what you want, Dorethea, then so be it. Is that truly what you want?"

I knew she was hoping to change my mind. "Yes," I told her, "being a farmer's wife is what I truly want."

That is how it was. Though Mama finally acquiesced to my wishes, she wanted to arrange a lavish wedding next summer in Richmond with everyone she knew in attendance. I told her I'd have none of it. John Forbes and I are to be married in Bethel Church next month with only the immediate family and neighbors as witnesses. His mother will play the piano for us and Uncle Ezra will give me away. I almost told Mama we had decided to get married on horse-back, but decided better of it.

She would have been *quite scandalized*.

Chapter 5
UNCLE HENRY

CONFESSION
GOOD FOR THE SOUL

Dear Lawd.

I'uz a ol' man an' ready to go if you see fit for Yo' will to be done on earth as it is in heaven. I had me a dream las' night that I take to be a sign.

I dream I'uz walkin' down the road 'twixt Penhook and Novelty, an' I seen a woman a little piece up the road from where I'uz walkin' an' she motion me to follow her. 'Course I'uz goin' that way anyhow. Little while later, she turn an' motion agin an' by that time I'uz close enough to see that she somebody I know, but I don't know jes' who. Well, we go on a piece more—she still out front ahead a me. We jes' about to the Novelty Depot by this time, an' she turn so I can see her face an' she motion to me agin. I see it Reeva—that who I been followin'. She been dead how long now? Thirty-some year. She turn down that road other side the depot an' I run to catch her but she jes' a little bit faster an' somehow I gittin' slower an' then a train come an' I got to wait on account she on the other side a the train. Train go past, an' I look for her, but she gone. I hear her voice callin' me.

"Come on, Henry," she say. "Come on."

Then I wake up an' I'uz tired jes' like I been runnin' a long way. I take it for a sign. I know it a sign.

I'uz ready to go, Lawd. I done live a long life an' I mostly been a dutiful servant—not only to You, Lawd, but to Mist' John Forbes an' his grandaddy Mist' Sam an' his daddy 'fore him, an' I ain't braggin' when I say ain't none of 'em ever complain.

I always work hard, go to church of a Sunday, an' do right. I been keepin' your commandments—least most a 'em.

I do thank you, Lawd, for always providin' me with enough to git by—always somethin' to eat, wood to burn in winter, shade trees in summer, always what I need.

I thank you for all the years you give me with Reeva.

I thank you for my home an' land an' the sense to stay on it when so many left theirs an' run off after the War.

I thank you for some mighty good times I had. An' for places I been I never think I'd see. I recollect one time me an' John Forbes an' that mare a his'n went to the fair. Fust fair we ever go to. I cain't recollect anymore jes' where it was, but it'uz a way off. Colonel Pemberton fix it so we'd go in a box-car on the train—fust time I ever rode all boxed up like that, an' that mare Joyful stompin' an' snortin' to beat all. We got to the fair, she seen all them other hosses an' she arch her neck an' prance jes' as purty. John Forbes he still a boy but he settin' on that mare like he somebody. Won us a blue ribbon, we did. John Forbes ridin' an' me the groom standin' at the rail watchin'. I brush an' polish on that mare til she shine. Folks clappin' they hands an' hollerin'. That'uz somethin'. Some folks want to buy that mare right then an' there. Pull out a big pocket-book full a money. John Forbes, he say no, she not for sale, not for nothin' you got. Been me, now I'da sold her. I'da been too tempted. I'uz always bad for temptation. Reckon you know that, Lawd, an' I'll git to that directly.

I look after that mare real good when John Forbes go off to that school where his daddy send him to study farmin'. All my life I been studyin' about farmin' but I done it on the farm. While he off, I breed that mare to a jack somebody down the road have, an' the next year I breed her again. John Forbes come back to take up farmin', he have him two good mules to start off with. One of 'em had a natchel rack jes' like the mare. Both of 'em jes' as red. Them mules somethin' to see. Good mules.

Now after John Forbes come back to stay, it won't too many year later that his daddy die an' his mama buy herself a house in

Rocky Mount an' start up with Miz Gillie Anne and Mist' Sam to come live with her. Her husband leave her right well off when he pass on. 'Course you know all this, Lawd, but it help me to go over it in my mind. Miz Julia she keep after 'em an' after 'em, an' soon they reckon they ready for a rest an' they know the farm in good hands. John Forbes marry Miz Dorie long about then an' bring her here to live. Miz Dorie about as fine a woman as you ever see. Mist' Sam an' Miz Gillie Anne live with Miz Julia 'til they pass on theirself, fust him one year an' then her the nex'. Both of 'em come home to be buried. They on the hill up here.

Now John Forbes an' me, we raise us a few more colts from that mare, an' it seem like each one better'n the one before. That'uz how we git that stallion Jubilation. He the fust one after them mules. Lawd, he a fine hoss! Big bay hoss with a white face. He by a big ol' Tennessee stud hoss belong to somebody Colonel Pemberton know. I hear Colonel Pemberton say, "You want a good hoss, you got to breed the best you got to the best you can git. Then you hope for the best." That what John Forbes done.

Folks all around brung mares to breed to that Jubilation. Pay right smart, too. 'Course, John Forbes he buyin' a few mares hisself now an' then to breed. Ever' year, we had us a good crop of colts to sell off—lotta hosses down toward Danville an' Halifax trace to Jubilation. We send a colt or two to Tennessee, maybe some to Kentucky. All of 'em—ever' one we raise—have that natchel rack jes' like that mare. Most a them colts jes' as red as red can be. A couple bays. Most red, though, with white markin's. John Forbes never sell the best ones. Those he keep. The mare Ever Joyful'uz one; her daughter Wild Joy 'nother'n. Bunch a ponies from Miz Dorie's little China Doll—kinda ponies rich mens buy for they little gals. Hosses an' ponies like you never did see. Purty hosses—might purty. Lawd, I know I in heaven if I hear hoof beats makin' that clickedy-clackedy rackin' sound when I git there.

I know heaven got hosses there, Lawd. "Then the gates of heaven open' and I beheld a white hoss whose rider was called

Faithful an' True," the Good book say. Don' say if the hoss racked, but I 'spec it did.

It Yo' will I reckon that hosses save this farm. Back when times was bad an' the two a us workin' could barely make a crop, we had them hosses. They bring money in. Long as folks farm, they gonna need a good hoss or mule. I reckon hosses one a Yo' best creations. For that, Lawd, I surely thank you.

Lawd, iff'n you can fix it, I would be right grateful iff'n I could ride Joyful 'round the Pearly Gates. She only been there a few years—I know she with You or it ain't heaven—so she know her way around. Mist' John Forbes set a great store by that mare. It hurt him right bad—him an' Miz Dorie both—when Joyful die. I'uz glad she don't suffer none. Jes' run up the hill one cold mornin' and drop in her tracks. Heart give out, I reckon. She'uz twenty-two, twenty-three. I done lost count. Not a mark on her when she die. When You see fit to take me, Lawd, I ain't mind goin' like that. Jes' drop in my tracks.

When Joyful die, Miz Dorie an' them two little gal babies start up cryin' all together. I help 'em bury that mare jes' like I help bury that mare's mama so long ago. Miz Dorie she stand up on the hill and sing "Bless Be the Tie That Bind"—that the purties' thing. That high clear voice she got somethin' to hear. Seem like the song hang in the air around you when she sing an' the air be all full a music. I know that voice she got one a Yo' gifts, Lawd. Like the Good Book say, make a joyful noise all ye lands.

When my time come, I hope there be singin'. Don't want nobody sad, want ever'body makin' a joyful noise.

So, Lawd, I'uz ready. I done made my coffin myself a year or two back outta some walnut planks. I got me a good suit wrapped up and laid away in the chiffarobe. I don't owe nobody nothin'. Mist' John Forbes he well enough off he can make do without me. I'uz gittin' too old to be much help nohow. I mus' be close to eighty-eight year old now from what Miz Dorie tell me. She say it all wrote down in a ledger she come across: "Baby boy born to slave girl Ester, 15 January 1817, baby to be name Henry if he live."

Patches on the Same Quilt

Well, Lawd, I 'spect I done live a mite longer than anybody think I would. Even me. I don' want to live so long I wear out my welcome. That why I say, You see fit, You take me anytime. I ready. I ready to see Reeva, an' them babies a hers that die when they so little, an' that mare. 'Course I want to see them Pearly Gates and them streets all pave with gold, an' St. Peter an' Jesus, and you too, Lawd. I reckon Reeva an' them babies all angels by now. That gonna be somethin', Lawd, if You can fix it—me ridin' that mare past the Pearly Gates with Reeva an' them babies flyin' longside. Now ain't that gonna be somethin' to see?

Well, Lawd, here I'uz askin' You for things an' I ain't got right with You. Oh, now I done been bab-tized when I'uz jes' a chap an' saved two-three times since. I reckon You know an' see all they is, so what I'uz fixin' to tell You ain't nothin' new to You, but I reckon it gotta be said. Confession good for the soul, the preacher say. What I'uz gonna tell You been a burden I been carryin' way too long. It'll be a relief to lay my burden down.

I confess that I lust after Odell Pangburn. It only happen the one time. I'uz a ol' man then—an' Odell won't no young thing, neither, though she considerable younger than me. I recollect it'uz late summer. I jes' carry John Forbes up to catch the train an' I'uz on my way back. I come up on Odell walkin' long the road totin' her things in a sack. She been helpin' birth a baby. That what she do, You recollect—birth babies. Done it all her life, jes' about. I ast her iff'n she like a ride, an' she say yes, she sho' 'preciate one. So I help her git in the wagon an' we ride on a piece. I stop at the crossin' an' let the mules drink. It a hot day. Odell look at me an' I look at her—one a them looks like we seein' each other for the fust time. Then she smile real shy an' lower her eyes. That the moment I start havin' feelin's I ain't have since Reeva die. I tell Odell I aim to take her home for supper. She say that be all right. She fix me a good supper an' then she stay the night. Nex' mornin' I wake up an' she gone. Jes' like she never been there. Jes' like I dream it.

Nex' year I see her totin' a baby.

"Whose chile is that?" I ast her.

"She my baby," say Odell. "Her name Rose-Ella."

"That chile mine? I the daddy?" I want to find out.

"Nossir," say Odell, "This chile all mine. She ain't got a daddy. I wait a long time for this baby, an' she mine an' only mine."

'Spite what Odell say, I know in my heart that I the daddy.

"I do right by you," I say to Odell, "if she mine."

"She ain't nobody's but mine!" Odell say agin. "An' that that!"

Now, Lawd, You and me both know that I gotta be the daddy a that chile, but Odell don't never say. That chile most a growed-up woman now, an' Odell never say.

'Bout nine-ten year after this chile born, Odell have 'nother one. She 'bout too ol' for bearin', but she do. I know nine month 'fore this'n come who the daddy is, an' it ain't me. But that somethin' else I got to confess, Lawd, on account I did a vengeful thing, an' the Good Book say, "Vengeance is mine saith the Lawd."

I recollect one Sat'dy mornin' it bitter cold. I git up 'fore daylight to stoke the stove up an' I hear a knock—"*peck, peck, peck*"—at the door. Now I ain't 'spectin' nobody, so I hesitate to open the door. There it go agin—"*peck, peck, peck.*"

I open up the door an' there stand Odell, her dress all tore up an' tears jes' runnin' down her face. One eye swole near 'bout shut an' some dry blood on her lip. She near 'bout froze, so I pull her in and shut the door an' fix her up some coffee. She warm up a mite, an' then she tell me what happen. It all come tumblin' out—ever'thing that happen—an' I feel right sorry for her.

She say she down below Peckerwood Level over to the Hubbler place the day before where Iretta Hubbler jes' have herself a baby. When ever'thing seem like it gonna be all right an' they don't need her no more, Odell git ready to leave. Silas Hubbler tell her when she git all her things, come on up to the barn an' he hitch up the wagon an' carry her on home. So she think that be all right an' she go to the barn. She git there, the wagon not hitched. Silas he reach out an' catch her by her arm an' pull her in a stall. She pull away an' tell him she don't do such as that. He tell her he reckon she do on account she got a chile an' never no husband. He smack her across her face an' throw her down. He a big man an' she cain't git loose. He hold her down an' force her. When he done, he hear his little boy cryin' an' callin' for his daddy. He turn loose a Odell an' go see about the chap. If that chap didn't cry, ain't no tellin' what Silas mighta done to Odell. She run off an' run all the way to my place. Say she don't want white folks to see her, so she come to me.

"You say if ever I need anything," she say, an' start up cryin'.

I'uz so mad my blood boil. I'uz ready to go git Silas Hubbler right then an' there, but Odell tell me no.

"He a white man," she say. "You ain't got no chance. Jes' give me time to git fixed up an' then you carry me home. I gotta git home to my little gal. She see me like this, she be afraid."

I heat Odell some water to wash herself an' give her needle an' thread to fix her clothes. I go out an' hitch up the mules while she fix herself up. After I carry her home, I study about what Silas Hubbler do to her. I study how to fix him good.

Well, Lawd, I reckon You an' me both an' ever'body in this end a the county know that Silas Hubbler make his livin' from the corn likker he make in that ol' tobacco barn down by the Pigg River. He got hisself a ol' cabin close by where most Sat'dy nights men git togither an' have a big time drinkin' an' carryin' on. They's a foot path through the pines you take to git there, but Silas got hisself a way out case the law slips up on him. He got a log 'cross the river for a bridge an' a piece a rope strung 'twixt two trees for a handhold. You can jes' barely see it from the road if you'uz to know where to look.

Now, a week or two after Odell come to me, I knowed there'uz gonna be a big time down at Silas's. I seen some men ridin' past an' I figger they goin' to drink theirselfs some likker. It'uz a miserable cold night with rain an' snow fallin' mixed together an' the wind jes' ablowin'. Kinda night a man might crave a drink to warm hisself up. I figger iff'n I'uz gonna fix Silas, then this the night to do it.

I slip on down to the barn an' saddle up one a Mist' John Forbes fastes' hosses. I took me a little saw along, too. When I git to the place in the road near that log, I tie up the hoss to a tree. Snow comin' down purty steady now. I saw that log up from the bottom where it don't show. Won't hard to do on account of that log bein' so rotted. Then I unravel that rope jes' a bit. While I'uz doin' this, I hear them men jes' a'laughin' and carryin' on. Before I git on the hoss, I pick up a good size rock from the bank. Then I climb on that hoss an' ride as close as I can git to that cabin. I fling that rock jes' as hard as I can where I think that cabin roof is. I hear it hit the tin an' roll off jes' a'clatterin'.

Ol' Silas holler, "Who thar?"

Then I kick that hoss an' ride jes' as hard as I'uz able. I hear a big crack an' a splash. Last thing I hear is ol' Silas cussin' somethin' fierce. That the fastes' I ever ride in my life, I reckon. Snow an' icy rain jes' a'pourin'. I don't stop til I git that hoss back to the barn an' dried off. Then slip on back home an' warm up my own self. I don't know iff'n I drown ol' Silas or not, Lawd, an' tell You the truth, I don't much care. I know that a sin, but I hope You see fit to forgive me on account Silas Hubbler don't die. Now, he'uz right sick for a right long spell. Too sick to force hisself on any woman, that for sure.

Week or two later, down at the store, I hear some men talkin' 'bout how ser'val men got pulled in the river when they try to haul Silas out. Serve 'em right. I cain't help it, Lawd, that jes' how I feel. Reckon You got to forgive me that, too.

I never tell a soul what I done—not even Odell. I figger Mist' John Forbes notice next day that his good saddle wet, but he never say one word about it. Won't long til law come an' chop up that still a Silas's. Not a thing Silas can do.

So, Lawd, I been keepin' this secret 'bout ten year or so. It feel good to let go a it an' confess to You. Feel like a load done been lifted.

Confession good for the soul, all right.

Now, Lawd, I'uz ready. I'uz ready....

Chapter 6
JULIA FORBES WEBSTER

WISHING YOU ALL THE BEST

1 November 1905
Rocky Mount, Virginia

My Dearest Dorie,

How delighted I was to receive your letter of Tuesday last informing me that you are once again in the family way. During my visit last summer, I felt as if you were, for you looked a bit peaked and seemed paler than your naturally fair complexion. I am so pleased that you decided to confide in me that you are expecting in March. Early spring couldn't be a better time for a baby to arrive. It is not yet hot and most of the bitter weather is long past. Spring is also a time of beginnings. I only regret that I will not be able to be with you at that time, but some months ago I made a commitment to play at the wedding of one of Charles' nephews in Baltimore. Knowing I would be there at that time, I also accepted some recital engagements in the area, so I expect to spend most of the month in Maryland. Of course, my heart and my thoughts will be in Virginia with you.

Tell John Forbes that he must engage Rose-Ella's services before the baby is due so that you may rest up during the last months of your confinement. She was such a help after Doreen and Little Julia were born. Whatever should we do without her?

If I have but one regret in life it is that I fear I shall not live long enough to see all my sweet grandchildren grow up and take their places in society. Now, Dorie, do not think for an instant that I fault you for this, for I most emphatically do not. We can only assume that it was God's will that you not be blessed with children during the first five years of your marriage. Think how much more precious the children were to us when they finally did arrive. No, the fault, if any, is my own. I fear I did not marry until rather late in life, for I was determined to see the world a bit first. Indeed, my early years at school at Botetourt Springs were well spent and I made many cherished friendships there. Then, there was the War. I was not the only young lady who had to postpone her search for a husband. I feel blessed that I was not among the many—as indeed several of my college chums were—who lost a sweetheart or fiance to the war. If anything, the War brought me my husband.

I don't believe I ever told you how Charles and I met. Let me set it down for you now that you may tell your children someday:

The spring after I was graduated from college, the War broke out and my younger brother John joined up. Why, it just wouldn't do until I could join in my own way, so when a good friend from college wrote me that she was working at Chimborazo Hospital in Richmond, I decided that was how I could also serve. Mother was, of course, opposed to the idea, but she knew it was useless to forbid me to do it, so she at length gave me her blessing. It was at Chimborazo that I met both your dear mother and my husband-to-be. Your mother, being of a fine Richmond family, contributed to the war effort and was able, by some means, to procure food for us when times were quite bad. But my husband—ah, that's another story altogether.

Just after the Battle of Cold Harbor, a young soldier with the bluest eyes I'd ever seen was admitted with a most embarrassing, for him, injury. A bullet had grazed him in a rather fleshy part of his anatomy before lodging in the cantle of his saddle, thereby spooking his horse, which reared and deposited him rather unceremoniously upon the ground. The impact broke the soldier's leg, a condition which rendered him quite unfit for battle for a period of several months. Fortunately, it was a very clean break and there were no complications.

Charles never cared to speak of this accident, for obvious reasons of male vanity, so I'm quite certain that John Forbes does not know the story. Since Charles, rest his soul, has been with the angels these dozen years, I believe the particulars can now be told.

But I'm digressing. At the hospital, Charles and I found we had many common interests—history and music being but two—and we became friends. When it came time for him to return to his regiment, he proposed to me, but I declined to accept at that particular time. Knowing he would be in the thick of fighting and fearing the worst, I bade him find me after the War was over and ask me again. I gave him directions to my parents' house—for that was where I should surely return, and he promised to find me.

He was a gentleman of his word. In mid-July following the surrender, my brother John, who often sat in the shade of the maple tree in the side yard, spied a stranger walking up the road. Fearing it might be a thief and being too weak from his war-time injuries, John summoned us, and we quickly assembled in the yard. My father held his rifle at the ready. There was much thievery after the War. We couldn't be too cautious. I remember it was a dry, dusty day and very hot.

I barely recognized Charles. He was covered with dust and had a scraggly beard. His clothing was torn and filthy. Only his clear, blue eyes were unchanged. When he saw me, he fell upon his knees and proposed marriage. Naturally, I said yes. Mother was fit to be tied. After he had cleaned up and trimmed his beard, she realized that he was indeed a gentleman of quality and she and Papa gave their blessings to the union. We were married within a few weeks and left on a wedding trip to southern Maryland where Charles' people lived.

My parents, I feel sure, expected us to return to Penhook after my brother's death, but Charles—who was certainly no farmer—was fortunate to get an appointment at the college in Salem, a mere fifty miles from my parents. There we lived quite happily for most of our married life, taking most of our summers and one glorious full year abroad. We had many wonderful travels, so I did indeed see the world, as I had long ago wished to do.

After Charles' fatal heart attack, it seemed wise for me to move from Salem to Rocky Mount, the better to be closer to family. The move enabled me to provide a comfortable home for my parents until their deaths and also offered me the opportunity to introduce new pupils to the joys of music. I was quite fortunate to find several willing piano students right here in Rocky Mount, so I have been quite busy teaching them. Every time one of my students learns a Mozart piano concerto, I think of you, for I know Mozart is your favorite composer. I am so pleased you allowed me to play several of his pieces at your wedding, though I am sure there must have been several in attendance who did not think this fitting wedding music. I am delighted that John Forbes plays Mozart for you so often. I look forward to the time when I can teach his music to little Julia. She should be ready to begin piano lessons by next year. During my last visit, she seemed so interested and her little fingers were almost strong enough when she sat on my lap, put her hands on top of mine, and "helped" me play. It is no small delight to me to see my namesake take such an interest in music. What a pity that Doreen is not similarly interested, but I believe, with proper encouragement, she will eventually develop an interest.

I do so look forward to seeing all of you again when I visit during Christmas week. Until then, do give my love and kisses to John Forbes, little Julia, and little Doreen. And please, Dorie, do take care of yourself. I feel quite certain that this time you shall have a little boy, though I won't be the least bit disappointed to get another precious granddaughter. Whatever it is, be certain that it is God's will. Bless you all.

Wishing you all the best, I remain,

Your loving Mother-in-law,
Julia Webster

Chapter 7
ANNIE PEARL

FORCED BLOSSOMS

I was young and pretty once.

Folks often said to me, "Annie Pearl, you can have your pick of any man in Union Hall."

Not that I had a regular beau, but there was several who smiled at me at church meetings and spell-downs and such. Mama said I was too young to be thinking about beaux; she needed me at home for a spell yet. Our family run to girls, and I was the oldest of four. I didn't realize when Mr. Webster come riding up on that fancy chestnut mare of his that he was the one.

He never asked me—he just assumed. Him and Daddy stood on the porch and talked first about the tobacco and horses and the weather. Then the talk turned to other things. I was across the yard at the shed. I was carding wool from the spring shearing, but I could make out most of what they said. They talked about Mr. Webster's children and what would become of them now their mama was dead. They spoke about what a fine young woman I was—how I was raised right and would make a good God-fearing wife and mother. I knew enough not to stare, but I caught glimpses. I saw Mr. Webster touch the corner of his moustache and look even more solemn; I saw Daddy nod. Then Mr. Webster mounted back up on his mare and turned her toward the road. He tipped his hat in my direction as he rode away, but he never spoke the first word to me.

Mama and Daddy called me to come to the house. Nobody asked me what I wanted. From the little window in the front room, I could still see Mr. Webster racking his mare up the path to the main road everybody calls the race-track.

Mama and Daddy said Mr. Webster was the one—he'd asked for my hand. They said I'd live in a big white-painted frame house on four hundred acres of prime land. This was my chance for happiness—they'd somehow make do without me.

He come in the wagon for me next day. He told Daddy not to worry; he'd respect me until the preacher come in two Sundays. It was just he needed me now—the garden was starting to come in, canning had to be done. His wife wasn't but two months dead, and his children needed a mama bad. The baby was sickly.

He didn't speak more'n a dozen words to me the whole five miles. When we got to his house, he set my valise on the front porch and went to the barn to unhitch the horse. I went on inside. It was a nice house. You could see from all the doodads and the piano and things it had a woman's touch. The colored girl he'd hired to tend his children looked at me and grinned.

"You got yo' work cut out for you, I reckon," she said, but not uppity—more like she just knew.

She handed me the baby boy. It was pale and thin—not like the rosy fat babies my sisters had been. Its mama had died having it.

Mr. Webster come in, paid the colored girl two dollars, and said, "Thank you, Rose-Ella."

She nodded to him, put on her bonnet, and flounced out the door and up the road; and I felt so alone. He showed me to the little room off the kitchen where I'd sleep with the two little girls. The little girls just looked at me with their big eyes and didn't say a word when he said, "Doreen, Julia—this is your new mama."

True to his word, he respected me. The two weeks passed in a kind of waking dream. Days were spent cooking and washing, shelling and canning the peas I'd picked in the cool of the morning, straightening up the house that had been let go for months, and tending the children's needs. The little girls were good children—you could tell they'd been taught proper—but the baby fretted and cried and wouldn't eat. The cow's milk didn't agree with it. I told Mr. Webster we needed a goat, and he

Patches on the Same Quilt

fetched one home the next day. The milk helped the baby some, but the goat was just one thing more to tend. I was always tired.

On meeting day, his mama come—a proud lady sitting straight on the buggy seat and clenching the reins with strong little bird-like hands. We sat for awhile in the front room and talked formal and polite. She looked at me hard, studying me. Finally she nodded to her son, and we loaded into the buggy and drove to Bethel Church.

When Preacher Martin looked into my face with his cold blue eyes, I felt like I was being looked at by God Almighty hisself.

I stammered, "I do," and it was done—for richer and poorer, better and worse, sickness and health, 'til death do us part. 'Til death.

Mama and Daddy come and spoke to me afterward like I was a grown person, but my sisters hung back like they didn't know me anymore. The little girls were used to me now and clutched my skirt and peeped out at my family. The baby cried.

We had no shivaree and no serenade. I reckon that was on account of him being married before and his wife not long dead. The little girls fretted when I moved the baby's cradle out of their little room and into the side room where their daddy slept.

Afterward—after we'd done what married people do—I couldn't sleep while he lay snoring. It was strange being next to a man. The little girls had snuggled against me like small, warm animals—but he turned away and kept to his own side. I got up and rocked the baby some. I kept thinking now I am a woman, and I know what other women know—but what did I really know?—I know once I was young and pretty, but now I felt so old, and it won't so long ago....

During June haying, neighbors come to help. The other women and I cooked and fetched water and visited in between the cooking and fetching. They talked of Dorie, his first wife, and how when she laughed it was like silver bells ringing. They said she was real pretty. I never saw her but once or twice—at Court Day in Rocky Mount—but I couldn't make a clear picture of her in my mind. I recollect her red hair. The oldest girl's got the same red hair. Dorie won't from around here. She come from Richmond, and she's still got people there.

When the last load of hay was in the barn and everybody had gone home, I felt lonesomer than ever.

In late summer, when tobacco time come, Mr. Webster hired some colored folks to help because the neighbors were all working their own tobacco. He was in and out of the house at odd hours—keeping the fires going to cure the tobacco just right—and I was always tired. The days and nights run together in my mind—I was always cooking or carrying water. He'd thank me for helping, but he treated me like one of the hired people, not like his wife. He still loves Dorie, I told myself.

When the wagons full of tobacco were finally loaded onto the flatcars for the train ride to Danville, he bade me good-by for a week. After the tobacco was sold, he aimed to look at some horse to buy while he was down there. My oldest sister come to stay with me—to help out and to keep me company.

A day after he'd gone, the weather turned right cold for September and a rainy spell set in. The baby took a turn for the worse. I don't generally hold with doctors—God's will is God's will—but I sent my sister to fetch one anyhow. The doctor did no good. The baby died. I found a little dress for it up in the attic amidst some of Dorie's things, and we fixed it up nice for the burying. Mr. Webster made it back from Danville in time to dig the grave hisself. He put the baby on one side of Dorie. I reckon the other side would be for him when his time come.

After the burying, he looked at me different—like he might look at a hound that didn't run true. He had me roughly that night and again the next. Then he didn't touch me for a long time and wouldn't hardly look my way anymore. All that fall and winter, he sat by the little window he'd had cut in the wall by the fireplace and watched Dorie's grave up on the hill.

I might have been young and pretty once, but I began to feel like an old woman. My body grew thick and I was sick mornings. I knew come early next summer I'd have a baby myself. Maybe it would replace Dorie's baby—maybe not.

In February there was a day when the air promised spring. The little girls and I were tired of being housebound. We walked up the road and gathered forsythia branches. We brought in an armload and put them in water in canning jars. A few days later, when winter had come back, the little girls smiled to see the branches filled with yellow bell blooms. The flowers wouldn't last, I knew—whatever blooms early fades fast, so I bundled up the little girls and we took the flowers up to the graveyard and put them on Dorie and her baby. That night snow fell and covered the flowers.

If he'd noticed what I did, he never let on. But he began to speak to me more and in a softer voice. Or maybe it was because I was getting so big, and he saw he had another chance for a son.

Spring finally did come, and the tilling and planting and all that goes with it. It was like the world started up fresh. I was always tired. I moved slowly and heavily through the long, busy days, trying to get my garden in and watch the little girls and keep the house clean.

One Saturday we all loaded into the wagon and went to Rocky Mount. My eyes hungered for the sight of other folks. When Mr. Webster helped me down from the wagon, I stood and stared and gawked more than was polite, then hurried the little girls on to get them some dress goods. They'd most out-grown ever'thing they had.

As I crossed the street to the store, I caught a glimpse in the window of a strange woman—her stringy hair flying loose from under her bonnet, her face reddened by wind, her awkward body swollen and heavy, two little girls clenched onto her faded skirt—and it was me that I gawked at. Had I changed so much in a year I didn't know my own self?

I went in the door. The store-clerk—a boy who just a year ago had smiled at me and would have talked to me if Daddy had let him—said, "Hello, ma'am," and didn't recognize me.

Was I ever young and pretty?

Chapter 8
DOREEN WEBSTER

LAY MY COMFORT DOWN

"My Autobiography," by Doreen Eugenie Webster. No. "Doreen E. Webster: Her Life and Times." Maybe "The Life of D. Eugenie Webster"?

Oh, I don't know. I just plain don't know.

We's supposed to write our autobiography for English class. That's a story of your life, an autobiography is. After you write it and hand it in, they put it in a folder in a filing cabinet in the office and keep it. Forever, I reckon. Every single person in the eighth grade has got to do it. That's always been the way at this school that Grandma—Grand*mother*—Cabell makes me go to ever since she brought me here to Richmond to live with her.

Only girls go to this school—not like back at our school in Penhook where both boys and girls in all the grades sat in the same room all together. This school even has a separate room for each grade except when the different grades get together—*assemble*—in a big room for special things. It's taken me some getting used to.

Grandmother Cabell told me she chose this school special because I'd meet fine young ladies from good families here, and they'd be my friends. This is not so. The girls act real polite when there are grown folks around, but when the grown folk ain't around, they make fun of the way I talk and tease me about my red hair. "Red head, red head, fire in the woodshed!" is one of the things they say, and hearing it makes me blush deeper than my naturally pink skin. They are not my friends and won't never be.

I get my hair and coloring from my mother who was Grandmother Cabell's only living child. I don't quite remember my mother, but used to tell my sister Julia that I did. When Julia was real little, she used to ask me did I remember our mama and I would always lie and say yes to make her feel better. It won't quite a lie—lying is a sin and you can burn forever and ever in hell for it—on account I remembered what other folks said about Mama.

How she had the most beautiful red hair. How she was always happy and laughing. How she could sing.

There's some things I really do recollect, but they's only pieces of things. There was a bird popping out of a clock on the front room wall and saying "Cuckoo!" over and over while someone—Mama, I reckon—tickled me and made me laugh. I remember hands on top of mine helping me pick out a tune on the piano while a voice sang "Do-Re-Me." I recollect being tucked under a quilt in the dark by someone who sang "Little Johnny Brown, won't you lay your comfort down?" and feeling like that comfort had been laid on me so I won't be scared of the dark. I recollect walking up a hill to the grave-yard holding Julia's hand in mine and her not big enough to keep up real good and asking, "Where's Mama at?" I remember yellow flowers on a grave in the snow. I don't know what I remember anymore.

At Grandmother Cabell's house there is a painting of my mama when she was a little girl. She has on a big straw hat with a yellow ribbon and she is swinging in a swing. She is smiling a big smile. Her hair is long and red.

"Auburn," says Grandmother Cabell, "auburn. Her hair was never red."

It looks red to me, though. Her cheeks are pink in the picture but the rest of her face is a light creamy color—not all-over pink like mine. I am not beautiful at all like she is and I never will be. Julia got the good looks. She is dark-headed like Papa and has his bluish-gray eyes with curly dark lashes. Ever'body always goes on about how pretty she is.

My little brothers, Johnny and Willie, look like Mama-Annie who has been my mama ever since I can remember—for a long time. Johnny was tow-headed when he was little. Then his hair

Patches on the Same Quilt

turned brown. Willie is still tow-headed. Maybe he will not change.

I miss them. I hope Johnny and Willie will not forget me the way I forgot Mama. They cried and cried when I got on the train with Grandmother Cabell. Papa held both Johnny and Willie—one in each arm—up high so they could both wave bye to me. Mama-Annie waved her handkerchief and dabbed at her eyes. Julia had hid and wouldn't come to the depot. I think she is jealous. That, or maybe she was afraid that Grandmother Cabell would grab her and make her come to Richmond, too, even though she promised Papa that she would only take one of us.

Grandma Julia—the one my sister is named for—didn't come to see me off either. She had said her good-byes a few days before when she gave me the quilt for a keepsake. She had drove all the way from Rocky Mount in her buggy to give it to me. She said she'd not come to the depot on account it is bad luck to watch someone until they're out of sight. If you do it, they might not come back. She made me stay in the house when she got in her buggy and drove off. Daddy and Mama-Annie watched me, though—they stood on the platform and waved and waved until they were just little specks. I thought I was a grand lady the way they saw me off, but later I got sad and I ain't got over it yet. Grandmother says I will, but I have found that she is not always right. I don't dare tell her, though.

The quilt is on top of the chiffarobe in my room. It's folded up in a box. Grandmother Cabell says I can't put it on my bed on account it don't go with anything. It is too plain and country-looking for Richmond, is what she means.

My room in Richmond which I have all to myself has wallpaper with pink roses and the coverlid on my bed is pink too, and slippery. It has lace all around the edges. The curtains are pink and have lace, too. It looks like the room of a great lady. It was Mama's room when she was little.

My quilt is cream-colored cotton on one side and all different color patches on the other. My Great-grandma Gillie Anne Forbes made it the year before she died.

Grandmother Cabell took one look at the quilt and shook her head and pursed her lips.

"The colors don't even go together," she said, and shook her head again. "Some of the patches are even faded. Whatever was she thinking of to give you such a thing?"

I was afraid she was going to give it to the poor children. That's what she did with most of my clothes, even though I tried to explain that I always passed my clothes down to Julia when I got too big for them.

Instead, she boxed the quilt up and put it on top of the chifforobe. For a few weeks, I got it out every night and laid it over me so I could go to sleep. I woke up early every morning just like I used to—even though there's no rooster in Richmond like on the farm—so I had time to fold up my quilt and box it up again before Grandmother suspected. Ever so often, I still take it out and wrap up in it. It feels so soft and good.

When Grandma Julia gave it to me, she pointed to the different patches and told me about each one.

"This one's out of your mama's wedding dress," she said as she fingered a pale green piece, "and this one's out of the dress she wore the day she met your daddy, and this plaid one's a piece of one of my old recital dresses, and this gray wool one is from your Great Uncle John's Confederate uniform, and...." she went on and on. She told me about every piece of that quilt.

"I'm giving you this because you're the oldest girl," she said to me. "I was going to give it to your mother, but she became an angel before I could do it. It's a keep-sake. Someday, you can pass it to your daughter and tell her all about it, so she'll know where she came from."

What she didn't tell me was about the back of the quilt. About the plain side. Only it won't plain.

One day I noticed on that side something about the lines that the thread makes where it is quilted to keep the cotton batts inside from wadding together. When you first look at it, you think it is just plain common thread. But if you study it closer, you can see that the stitches make pictures and words. Just like somebody drew the pictures or wrote the words with thread. I found the names "Forbes" and Webster" wrote several times, and "John Forbes Webster wed Dorethea Eugenie Cabell" and

"28 July 1895" and "John Robert Forbes—6 Oct. 1840—12 Sept. 1865," among others.

And pictures. There is a shape of our house and the big maple along side it. And a piano like the one in the front room that nobody is allowed to play but sometimes Julia does. And a horse that must be Papa's first mare Old Joyful because knotted thread makes a spot on its face. And another horse that don't look quite right on account one hind leg is not stitched very good. And a girl on a pony that looks something like my pony Dollbaby, only Dollbaby won't born when this quilt was stitched. There's a Confederate flag. And lots of other things. I can run my finger over the threads and feel these pictures even in the dark. It is a great comfort to me when I miss home so bad I almost cry.

Grandmother says I am too big a girl to be a cry-baby and I must get over being homesick. That I must make Papa proud of me. I must learn to be a good Cabell. When I tell her I'm a Webster, she says "Blood will tell. "I do not know what that means. When school is over, she says, maybe we can go back for a visit. I do not tell her about the pictures on my quilt because they are not her things. They are mine and they make me recollect who I was. Who I am.

Grandmother has been telling me about the Cabell side of the family. She carried me over to Hollywood Cemetery where lots of people who ain't even kin to each other are buried. It don't even look like a graveyard, which is what a cemetery really is. It is way too big and has statues and benches and things. Some families is buried with one another, but beside of them might be total strangers. I do not much like the idea of laying among strangers through all eternity 'til Judgment Day. The Cabell part has a iron fence around it. Even though Hollywood Cemetery has got pretty grave markers and big trees and is right along side of the James River which is much bigger than the Pigg River ever was even when flooded, I like our family graveyard up on the hill whole lots better. I would never say this to Grandmother.

I think it might be that Grandmother is sorry that Mama won't buried in Hollywood Cemetery inside the pretty fence, but I am glad she is in our family graveyard where she belongs next to my little baby brother. One day ever' year, Grandma Julia and

Mama-Annie clean off the graveyard and Julia and me help pull weeds. We take a box lunch up on the hill and spend the whole day. Grandma Julia always tells us about ever'body up there. Other times, Mama-Annie takes flowers up there sometimes and I help her and I put flowers on Mama. Who would put flowers on her in Hollywood Cemetery?

Grandmother showed me pictures of Mama when she was a young lady like she wants me to be. They's in a velvet covered book in the front parlor. Sundays we sit in there. One of the things a lady can do Sundays is to look at that book. She has got another book with all the Cabells wrote down in it. All the ones from the first one in 1684. The book has Mama in it and my name and Julia's and the day we each was born. The last name ain't a name at all. It just says, "Infant boy b. 7 March, died 30 Sept. 1906." That would be my little baby brother.

"Where's Johnny and Willie's names?" I asked the first time I saw that book. I thought maybe she forgot to write them in.

"They don't belong. They're not Cabells," Grandmother said. "That is the reason their names are not entered."

There is not much else to do in Richmond on Sundays if you's studying to be a lady. Sunday mornings we ride in the carriage to the Episcopal Church which is what Grandmother wants me to join, even though I told her I am a Baptist and have been saved and baptized and washed in the blood of the lamb. She tells me I will change my mind when I see the light. I seen all the light I care to see. The preacher wears something that looks like a dress, and you can hardly call what he does preaching at all.

After church we come home and eat dinner which Bertha the cook serves to us in the dining room. After that we sit in the parlor. I am allowed to read if it is a proper book or the Bible. Needlework is all right, too, but I ain't real good at it. It is not much like real sewing, which is a sin to do on Sunday but which is more useful than needlework. If I knew how, I could play the piano. Grandmother was shocked when I told her that I won't taught how.

"But your father plays!" she said.

Patches on the Same Quilt

"No, ma'am,' he don't," I told her. "Ain't nobody uses our piano except when Grandma Julia visits."

I didn't mention how my sister Julia slips and plays it sometimes. I don't reckon it's a lie if I don't tell something that ain't supposed to be done, is how I see it.

"He used to play," she told me. "He used to play every day for Dorethea."

I did not remember that.

Another lady-like thing to do on Sundays is to write. Usually I write to Julia and sometimes she writes back. On Sunday afternoon, I know, she is out riding Dollbaby or helping tend the boys while Mama-Annie fixes dinner, or else she is riding in the buggy with Papa to visit somebody or maybe look at a horse. Papa will let her stand in front of him and take the reins and play like she is driving. I know that she is doing these things on account they are the things I used to do, too. When I didn't have to be a lady and could just have a good time.

The first Sunday I was here in Richmond and did not know not to, I went to the kitchen and asked Bertha if I could be of any help. She said I sure could and was tying a apron around me when Grandmother came in and grabbed me by the arm and pulled me into the dining room.

"What is the matter with you?" she said. "You are not to bother Bertha when she is working!"

"It won't a bother," I told her. "I was fixing to help her."

I felt proud that Mama-Annie had raised me right to help other folks.

"A lady does not do domestic work!" she said. "And you are not ever to socialize with the domestic help. Besides that," she said, lowering her voice to almost a whisper, "Bertha is *colored!*"

People's ways is different in Richmond. I did not tell Grandmother that no one ever fussed at me when I was little and used to try to help old Uncle Henry pull weeds in his garden. Ever'body spoke nice to Uncle Henry and he was just as colored as Bertha. He is even buried on our place. I wonder if Bertha will be buried in Hollywood Cemetery with the Cabells. I do not think she will.

Grandmother asks me why I do not invite my little friends from school to visit on Sundays. I tell her that I do not have any friends at school.

"Oh," she says, "but you must cultivate their friendship. They are from such fine families."

If I told her how mean they really are and how they tease me, she would not believe it. I tell her that I will see about it.

Because today is Sunday, I am trying to write that autobiography for school. I simply do not know what to say. I have not done a whole lot in my life worth writing about. Grandmother suggested putting in all the important Cabells from her book who came before me. But I do not know them. They ain't—*are not*—my people. She just wants me to put them in so the teachers will see and know that I am somebody. It is important to Grandmother that other people think I am a lady. There is no use of me trying to talk to her about it because her mind is made up.

When Grandmother is busy with her needlework, I will slip upstairs to my room and wrap myself up in my quilt. I will hum to myself so soft that Grandmother won't hear, "Little Johnny Brown, won't you lay your comfort down," and I will play like I am taking a nap so nobody will bother me and I can think my own thoughts. I will study about what I can write, and when I am good and ready I will come back downstairs to the parlor and try my best to be a fine young lady.

I will try my best.

Chapter 9
YOUNG JULIA WEBSTER

WHEN IN ROME

When I look back now, my life seems just like a fairy tale. I left in disgrace to go out in the world to seek my fortune, I married a handsome prince, and I even had the help of a fairy godmother. Well, perhaps Tarlie wasn't a prince, but he was handsome and rich and kind; and perhaps Grandma Julia wasn't really a fairy godmother, but she was the next best thing, and she opened doors to worlds that I could hardly imagine, and I'll be forever grateful to her for giving me the life I've led—a happy life that any fairy-tale princess would envy.

You can ask anyone in our end of the county—Penhook or Union Hall or Novelty—and they'll tell you: "Oh, yes, Julia Eustacia Webster? Why, she went off to New York City and married her a rich man and became a great lady."

That's what they'll say. They won't tell you the leaving home in disgrace part. Only one person alive besides me knows it, and she'll take that secret to her grave. I don't even think about it much myself—it was so long ago and far away that sometimes I believe it happened to some one else, not to me at all.

When I was little, my sister Doreen and I were as close as ever two sisters could be. We did everything together—slept in the same big bed, played doll-babies in the shade of the side-yard maple tree, raced our ponies across the hayfields, picked blackberries in summer for Mama-Annie—our step-mother who'd raised us just as if we were her own—to make blackberry cobbler, walked back and forth to school, helped Mama-Annie look after little Johnny and Willie, went with Papa to buy and sell horses—we'd ride the ponies for him to show prospective customers how gentle and mannerly they were—and then we'd cry together when the ponies were sold. We did everything together. Sometimes, we'd talk about our real mama, although neither of us could remember very much, and we'd pick armloads of flowers—daisies and Queen-Anne's lace and Joe-Pye weed—and take them up the hill and put them on her grave. Then we'd sit up there and talk about how when we grew up we'd marry brothers and how our children would play together and how when we were very, very old, we'd be buried up here and our great-grandchildren would come and put flowers on us. The idea of dying never bothered us. It was just something you'd eventually get around to doing. Everybody did, sooner or later. Life was predictable like that.

One day everything changed. Our Grandmother Cabell, whom we rarely saw, wrote Papa a letter saying she was coming to visit for a while.

"I desire," she wrote in an elegant hand on stiff rose-colored paper, "to renew the acquaintance of my precious granddaughters."

Mama-Annie like to tore the place apart house-cleaning it for the better part of a week. Not that our house was dirty—Mama-Annie kept it spotless—but this was a special occasion. Doreen and I helped. We polished every inch of wood furniture in the house at least twice. It was like we were getting ready to welcome a great king or queen or somebody.

On the day Grandmother Cabell was supposed to arrive, Mama-Annie scrubbed us so hard our faces hurt and made us put on new-ironed dresses before she'd allow us to go with Papa to meet the train. Mama-Annie wouldn't go with us. She said it wasn't fitting since she wasn't blood kin. Besides, she said, she'd need to stay and look after the boys and get dinner.

Papa hitched up his two best horse—high-stepping matched sorrel geldings—to the buggy. He'd put on a tie and a vest and his suit coat, even though the weather was hot. He drove slow to the depot so as not to sweat up the horses. When we got there, we waited on the platform for the train to pull in. With the weather so hot, it seemed to take forever. Finally, we could hear the train way off. A few minutes later, it huffed and puffed in. We held our ears, it made so much noise. The train stopped and the conductor got off first and put down a little step. Then Grandmother Cabell got off and saw us standing there. She swept toward us—toward Doreen, rather.

"Dorethea," she said, reaching and stroking Doreen's red hair. "I'd know you anywhere!"

Doreen didn't know to say. She could only stand and stare at Grandmother Cabell's fine clothes. Doreen always did tend to be bashful.

"Her name's Doreen," I said. "I'm Julia," I added, just in case Grandmother Cabell might have forgotten. Unlike Doreen, I was never one to be at a loss for words.

Grandmother Cabell stared at me as if I were an intruder. Maybe she didn't care for my unruly black curls that Mama-Annie had tried so hard to comb straight, for she didn't touch my hair. I had dark hair like Papa, only his is straight. I have his blue-gray eyes, too. Doreen's eyes are green. I noticed that Grandmother Cabell's were the same green. I wondered if her white hair had ever been red, but I knew it would be impolite to ask.

Papa gathered up her baggage which the conductor had set upon the platform and put it in the buggy. He helped Grandmother Cabell into the back seat. She patted the seat beside her and told Doreen to come sit next to her. I climbed in front with Papa, where I would rather be anyway, but I couldn't help but feel slighted. Everyone one else had always treated me and Doreen exactly the same. I couldn't hear very well what Grandmother Cabell was saying to Doreen from where I sat because of the clatter of the horses' hooves. Papa made them step out smartly at a fast rack so they'd look stylish. It didn't matter now if they did sweat. Every so often, he'd look at me and smile. I think maybe he wanted to get home fast. So did I.

Mama-Annie had out-done herself for dinner. Her garden had come in good this year,s and the table was loaded with fine things to eat. She'd used the plates she'd brought down from the attic—plates I'd never seen before the other day when she'd taken them out of a dusty trunk she'd pulled from way back

79

under the eaves. Doreen and I had followed her up the steep steps. We hardly ever went to the attic by ourselves. It was dark and hot under the tin roof in summer, bitter cold in winter—not at all a pleasant place to play, despite all the treasures that were hidden there. I think we believed that old ghosts lived up in the attic. While Mama-Annie was busy finding the plates she wanted in the trunk, Doreen and I found a lot of old clothes that we wanted to claim for playing dress-up, but Mama-Annie said we weren't to have them. Doreen and I then busied ourselves with peeping into another trunk where we found a big carved clock. We wanted to take it down and hang it in the front room, but Mama-Annie made it clear we weren't to touch it or anything else in that particular trunk.

"Someday soon enough it'll be yours," she said, "but not yet. Your Papa would be unhappy to see that clock hanging on the wall downstairs. It would remind him of things best forgotten. You wouldn't want to make him unhappy, would you?"

We shook our heads no. There were other things we knew about that would make Papa unhappy. One was the piano in the front room. Though I longed to open it and put my fingers on the keys and make sounds come out, I was not allowed to—at least not when Papa was within hearing distance. It would make him unhappy. The only times the piano was opened was when Grandma Julia came to visit, which was often but not often enough to suit me, and Papa happened to be away from the house. Grandma Julia could make the most beautiful music come from that piano. It made me proud to be named for her. She would always open the hinged wooden cover over the keys ever so carefully and then adjust the stool to suit her and then she'd play. She'd play such pretty music it made me happy just to stand there beside her and listen. I couldn't for the life of me understand why it would make Papa sad. No one would tell me why.

"Some things are better not talked about," Mama-Annie would say, and that was that. No use arguing. But Mama-Annie'd never say a word to Grandma Julia when she placed my hands on the keys and taught me the scales and some simple tunes. I caught on fast. Doreen had never been especially interested in the piano.

"Someday, you'll be a great pianist," Grandma Julia once whispered to me, "and people will come from far and wide to hear you play. You'll be a great lady."

I never forgot her words. They were a great comfort to me many times, especially when Grandmother Cabell slighted me. Maybe Doreen was as jealous of Grandma Julia's attention to me as I was of Grandmother Cabell's attention to her, but Grandma Julia was always nice to Doreen. She always offered to include her. Doreen simply lacked interest.

Every time I went to Rocky Mount to visit Grandma Julia, usually on Court Days when Papa had business to take care of, she gave me lessons. Before long, I could play whole selections by heart. I never let on to Papa that I could play. Even on the long ride home, when he'd ask me how I spent my time, I never told him. It was my secret, and it was enough that Grandma Julia and I knew. Doreen knew, too, but she never told. I'd have kept her secrets, too, if she had any. We were sisters, and sisters do that.

Grandmother Cabell hadn't been with us more than a few days when she cornered Papa and sprang some news on him. They were sitting in rockers on the front porch one evening about dusk. I was in the side yard and, from behind the big maple tree, could hear most of what they said, but they couldn't see me. Doreen was still in the kitchen. It was her turn to help Mama-Annie wash the dishes and do up the night work.

"John Forbes," said Grandmother Cabell to Papa, "I desire to have Doreen accompany me on my return to Richmond. I can give her every advantage."

"No," said Papa. I was proud of him.

Grandmother Cabell's voice got sharper. "You owe me," she said. "You robbed me of my only daughter. She would have enjoyed all the advantages of her position in Richmond. Instead, you kept her in this God-forsaken backwoods county to die."

Papa didn't say anything for a long while. I dared not even breathe for fear they'd hear me. I knew I wasn't supposed to be listening. It was nearly dark. I could hear a whippoorwill call far off. Finally Papa spoke.

"She was happy here," Papa said in a tight voice that didn't sound like him at all. "She was happy here. We loved each other."

"Happy? Loved?" Grandmother Cabell replied. "Whatever does that have to do with anything? If you feel you owe me nothing, then certainly you owe her. At least give her child a chance to be what Dorethea would have been—should have been—herself."

"But Doreen's *my* daughter, too," Papa protested.

"And you still have another one left," answered Grandmother Cabell. "I shan't take both. I'd not leave you childless—" her voice broke off. She inhaled deeply and started again. "At least let me ask Doreen if she'd like to go."

Papa finally agreed. I heard him go into the house and come back with Doreen. Then he walked off in the direction of the barn. I knew he was going to check the horses. He always checked the horses if something bothered him. I was torn between wanting to run after him and wanting to stay and listen. Listening won out. I didn't dare move even though it was now black dark and I couldn't be seen. Try as I might, I couldn't quite make out all that was said. Grandmother Cabell spoke in a low, soft voice now, not like the one she used to Papa. All I could plainly make out were Doreen's occasional "Yes, ma'am's." Hidden by the dark, I crept around the side of the house to the back porch, climbed the steps, and went in through the screen door. A few moths clung to the screen. Mama-Annie had lit the lamps, and the glow of them promised warmth and safety.

Mama-Annie's ample backside was to me as she finished her night work. I went to her and hugged her.

"Why, Julia," she said as she turned around, "what on earth—?" She looked at my face and laid the back of her hand on it. "Law, child, you're burning up. You go on up to bed and I'll be up directly."

I did what I was told without a word. I didn't need a lamp to light my way up. I'd been up the steps so many times I could easily find my way. A few minutes later, after I had slipped between the sheets, Mama-Annie came in with a cool wash-rag and sponged me off. It was a long time after Mama-Annie left that Doreen came in. I didn't say anything, but even in the dark she knew I was awake.

"I'm going to Richmond to stay with Grandmother Cabell a while," she said. "I'll write you every day 'til I get back."

I said nothing and played like I was asleep. Maybe she doesn't know, I thought. Maybe she doesn't know it will be always and forever. I stayed way to my side of the bed with my back to Doreen, and she lay with her back to me. I wondered, as I lay unable to sleep, if she couldn't sleep either, but I made up my mind not to speak a word.

The next morning, I saw Grandmother Cabell's cameo pinned to the front of Doreen's dress, and I knew she'd been bought and paid for with the promise of more pretty things to come. In the days following, it seemed like Doreen was always by Grandmother Cabell's side, and there was no room there for me. I felt as if a space opened up between Doreen and me, a space too big for me to jump across, and I was left standing by myself. I was confused as to why this happened, but one thing I knew clear—we would never again be as close as we'd been before this week.

A few days later, when Grandmother Cabell and Doreen were ready to leave, I ran off and hid in the hay-loft and wouldn't come down to go with everybody to take them to the depot. I refused to even say good-by. This time, Papa had mules hitched to the wagon. With Mama-Annie and Johnny and Willie going, the buggy would have been too crowded. Then, too, maybe Papa didn't feel any need anymore to impress Grandmother Cabell with high-stepping horses.

After they'd gone, I sneaked back into the empty house like a thief and climbed the steep attic steps, I opened the forbidden trunk and looked through it. There were some old clothes, small lacy ones like a baby'd wear, and an embroidered sampler that was so silky-delicate I feared it might fall into shreds in my hands. I read the words stitched in dainty faded thread: "We might not be cut from the same cloth, but we're all patches on the same quilt." I put it back and lifted out the clock. I let my fingers fiddle with the hands and the pendulum while I studied the carving. A bird popped out and hollered, "Cuckoo!" and frightened me so bad it was all I could do to get the clock back in the trunk and the trunk-lid closed. I was sure the attic-ghosts were near and had sighted in on me. I ran down the stairs, almost falling in my haste. I dared not look back.

I didn't want to wait alone in the house for everyone to get back—everyone except Doreen and Grandmother Cabell. I sat in the swing on the front porch and let my mind run back over events from the past week. First thing the morning after I'd pretended I was asleep, Doreen had started to act like she was a queen or something. I purely couldn't stand it. To give me something to do, Mama-Annie had me take a note up to our tenant-man telling him to carry me up to Penhook to the store so I could have Mr. Dooley use his telephone to call Grandma Julia and tell her about Doreen. She gave me some money tied up in the corner of a handkerchief. Grandma Julia had a telephone in her house. We did not. The store was the closest place that had one. It took the better part of a morning for me to do the errand. Buck, our tenant-man, seemed to make the mules walk extra slow. In Richmond, I realized, Doreen would have a fancy carriage. I had mules. It was another thing I had to feel sorry for myself about. After Mr. Dooley had gotten through to Grandma Julia and read what was on the note, he put down a box for me to stand on to reach the mouthpiece and handed the ear piece to me.

"You tell everybody I'll be there tomorrow afternoon," Grandma Julia told me. I said I would, but I didn't tell until late that evening, sending Mama-Annie into a dither, trying to get the already-clean house spotless again.

Grandma Julia came, bringing a big package, a going-away present for Doreen. All she had for me was a promise to come get me and take me to visit her before long. She stayed the night, then left early the next morning. She had piano students expecting her, she said.

The rest of the week, Mama-Annie and Doreen tried to decide which of Doreen's clothes to pack, though Grandmother Cabell said not to bother. She'd get Doreen new things in Richmond. Doreen, it seemed like, was getting everything and I was getting nothing. With my nose so out of joint, I didn't have much to say to Doreen all week. Not that I'd have a chance to say it anyway. Mr. Dooley told near about everyone in the county who came into the store that Doreen was going to Richmond, so we had a steady stream of neighbors stopping to see her before she left.

Then she was gone. Papa and Mama-Annie and Johnny and Willie came back without her. I didn't speak a word to a soul for the next three days, but nobody else talked much either. It was as if Doreen had died, and we were in mourning. Finally, Grandma Julia broke my silence by appearing suddenly one morning and taking me back with her to Rocky Mount. I played her piano as much as I wanted, striking the keys with a strength and vengeance I didn't know I possessed. When she gave a lesson to one of her students, I stood off to the side and watched, my fingers moving as if I were taking the lesson myself.

When I started playing more temperately, Grandma Julia took me home—but it wasn't home anymore with Doreen gone. She'd only written me one letter in the two weeks since she'd gone, but it was short and newsless, mostly about things she'd seen from the train. Part of me had been cut off, it seemed like, removed to somewhere I couldn't reach, and no matter where I looked, I couldn't quite find myself.

"Just let her be," I over-heard Mama-Annie say to Papa one morning. "When school starts up next week, she'll have something else to think about."

I discovered then that I could do just about anything I wanted—within reason—and no one would stop me. That was when I took to going off for long rides on my pony, exploring places I'd never been, as if I were searching for something. After a few remarks about my gallivanting all over the county, Mama-Annie didn't say much about my wanderings. Papa never said anything in the first place. He knew that I was a good rider and, as long as I stayed on my pony, no harm was likely to befall me. Besides, everyone knew me. Any misdeeds I might have considered would have been duly reported to Papa. Then school started, my ramblings ceased, and I buried myself in my books.

Doreen wrote dutifully for a while, but her letters became increasingly less frequent and began to sound as if they'd been written by some stranger who'd replaced my sister. Months later, when she came home for Christmas, she was indeed a stranger to me. I knew then we'd never marry brothers or raise our children together or live happily ever after. I knew my sister—who'd been my dearest friend in the whole world—was indeed as lost to me as if she'd died.

When school was dismissed in the spring, I once again took up my habit of riding off for hours at a time. Since I was rapidly out-growing my pony, Papa gave me the job of riding whichever young horse needed working before it was ready for sale. As long as I completed my house chores, Mama-Annie made few comments.

"Tain't fittin' for a young woman to go gallivantin' all over goodness-knows-where by herself," was her most frequent complaint, but she was glad enough whenever I rode to do her errands—to take eggs to the store to sell, take a mess of greens from her garden to a neighbor, go to the post office and bring back news of how the war in Europe was going. Despite Mama-Annie's most frequent worry, "What will the neighbors think?," if anyone thought my solitary jaunts weren't "fittin'," they never said so to my face. I continued my rides for the next few years.

My disgrace came when I was sixteen, and Mama-Annie was the first to know. That year, 1918, Papa had an especially skittish filly, but I was confident of my abilities to handle her. One especially hot day in early June, I decided that I'd head down toward Peckerwood Level, along the road by Pigg River. It was shady and cooler there. The filly had been pulling at the bit stronger than usual so, despite Papa's warning, "Don't let the horse run—it ruins the rack," I let her have her head. She took off. It was a thrill to feel her running flat out, the trees whizzing past us and my hair flying. While I felt momentarily guilty for disobeying Papa's warning, it was too much fun to stop. Besides, who'd see to tell him? The road through this part of the county was not heavily populated.

Suddenly the filly did stop, so suddenly she reared and dropped me off her back. When she was free of me, she turned

Patches on the Same Quilt

and ran for home. I lay there, sprawled in the dust, my pride hurt more than anything else for I was rarely unseated by a horse. Then I heard laughter above me, and looked up to see a dark-haired boy on the over-hanging limb above me. I rose and tried to salvage my dignity.

"Just who do you think you are, spookin' my horse like that?" I demanded. I wasn't completely sure he had spooked the horse, but it was a distinct possibility.

"Ain't my fault you cain't ride," he said and smiled.

I noticed his eyes were as dark as his hair. He had freckles across his nose, and nice teeth that showed when he smiled. He dropped from the limb in an easy motion like he'd done it often.

"Who are you?" I demanded. I looked him straight in the eye. "What is your name?"

"Eben," he said. "Eben Hubbler." He met my gaze head on. "And I reckon I know who you are. Ever'body knows who your daddy is."

It was then I realized who his daddy was—old Silas Hubbler, and everybody knew who he was, too.

"You're never to talk to them trashy Hubblers," Mama-Annie had cautioned me once when we saw some of them on the road. "Silas Hubbler makes likker."

Mama-Annie was against whiskey-drinking and wouldn't have whiskey in the house. If she saw Hubblers in public, she looked right past them, as if they weren't even there.

"How am I going to get home now?" I wondered aloud.

Eben smiled again. I didn't know what he had to smile about. He had a nice smile, though.

"Wait right here,' he said. "I'll see what I kin do."

He waded across the river and disappeared into a pine thicket. I heard voices—his and his daddy's, I reckon—but except for a few curse words from the older voice, I couldn't make out what they were saying. Finally, Eben came back, astride one of the sorriest-looking mules I'd ever seen.

"Come on," he said, offering me his arm, And swung me up behind him. He was awfully strong for a skinny boy. "You best hold tight," he added.

I put my arms around his waist. His overalls were dirty and, I could see close up, a ring of dirt circled his neck. I could smell his sweat. He kicked the mule into a trot. I held on tighter to keep from bouncing off. All Papa's riding stock was smooth-gaited. I'd never been on a trotting animal before and I didn't like it. I thought my teeth were like to jar out.

I made Eben stop and let me off before we got to our road. I knew I'd be in enough trouble without having to explain why I was sitting behind a Hubbler on a mule. I slid down and politely thanked Eben.

"Might be I'll see you agin?" he asked.

I didn't answer. I could feel his eyes watching me as I walked away.

When I reached the barn, Papa was currying the filly. He said nothing, waiting for the explanation that was due him.

"She threw me," I said. "I couldn't catch her."

"Where?" he wanted to know. "What happened?"

"Down the road apiece," I said. "Something in a tree must have spooked her." That much was the truth.

I was glad he didn't ask how I'd gotten home. I let him think I walked.

The next day, I rode a different horse. I knew I ought not, but I rode down toward the river. Eben was astride the mule and waiting by the side of the road. He rode along with me for a piece. He was there the next day and the one after that. I knew I shouldn't keep going down that way, but it seemed like I couldn't help it. Sometimes, after I left Eben, I ran the horse to Penhook and made sure somebody at the post office or store saw me before I went back home. Papa was busy with his tobacco and the horse-breeding business. His mind was on the war in Europe, and he figured the army was using so many horses and mules that folks in America would soon need replacements. He'd bred every mare on the place and was making arrangements to buy more brood-mares. He traveled all around looking for stock. He kept his mind on that, not on what I might be doing. Mama-Annie had her usual big garden and her canning to do. My brothers were at the rambunctious age—old enough to be a big help to Papa, but also old enough to know their own minds—and Mama-Annie's attention was on making sure they did their chores, lest they slip off and get into trouble. My tracks were covered should anybody be tracking me, but nobody was.

One day in mid-July, when all the trees were heavy green and a faint breeze blew, Eben told me he was joining the army. His two older brothers had already gone.

"I reckon we ought to say our good-byes," he said.

I didn't answer. He reached over and caught my gelding's bridle and led him across the river which was unusually low. We went through the stand of scrub pines and along a narrow path until we got to a clearing where the pine needles made a thick carpet on the ground. He lifted me off the saddle and tied my horse to one of the pines. My mind kept telling me, *this is wrong, don't do this*, but hadn't I known all along it was wrong to meet him? All I could think of for an excuse was that Doreen had left me and now Eben would, too

I felt Eben's lips press against mine and tasted what I suspected must be whiskey when I kissed him back. He kept kissing me, and then his hands started going under my dress. *This is wrong*, I thought again, but I kept kissing him back and losing myself in the kissing until it seemed that none of this was happening to me—it was happening to someone else, and I was far off watching, like the time Doreen and I once hid in the barn-loft and watched through a knothole when Papa bred his stallion to a mare.

Afterwards, Eben rode away and left me lying in the clearing. I waded into the river and tried to wash myself off, but it seemed like I would never be clean again. Eben didn't even say good-by. I raced the gelding home and turned him out still sweaty while I went inside to wash myself again. I didn't ever ride down that way ever again. I thought maybe if I didn't know that place was there, then nothing had ever happened.

Something had happened, though. A month later, I knew something was the matter with me. I'd always bled with the new moon. I watched the moon like I always did, but the new moon came and nothing happened. Then the full moon, then the last quarter. Nothing. No, not nothing—I started getting sick of mornings. Most times I could make it to the outhouse. One morning, when I couldn't and was vomiting into my chamber pot, I looked up to see Mama-Annie standing there. I'd not heard her come into my room, she was so quiet.

"When was you last bleedin'?" she demanded.

I told her. I saw her fingers move as she counted to herself.

"And the daddy? Who's the daddy?" she demanded next.

I told her I didn't understand. After she explained, I broke down and told her who I'd been with. She was quiet for several minutes. I dared not move.

"Well, what's done is done. Thank goodness, your papa's not here," she said at last. "He don't need to be troubled with this. You ain't to ever tell him!"

I nodded. Papa had left the day before for Tennessee to sell a gelding and look at some mares. He'd be gone a week, maybe two.

Mama-Annie had me follow her to the keeping room where she kept her chest of remedies. She unlocked the chest, took out a vial of laudanum, and had me take a dose. Then she told me to jump off the high side of the back porch. That might start the bleeding.

We tried the same remedy three days in a row, but the results were always the same.

"We need to do something before your papa gets back," she declared. "Your grandma will know what to do."

While she hitched up a gelding to the buggy, she had me get Johnny and Willie washed and dressed and ready to travel. Mama-Annie dared not call ahead from the store, for she didn't want anyone to know our business. She drove the gelding leisurely through Penhook, lest anyone wander why we were in a hurry, but once we were on the turnpike, she whipped him into a faster rack. Two hours later, when we turned onto Grandma Julia's street, the gelding was lathered and sweat poured down Mama-Annie's face. She got out of the buggy, tied the weary horse to the post, and told the boys to stay in the buggy or she'd whip them good. With me in tow, she strode to the door and banged on the heavy brass door knocker until Grandma Julia opened the door and invited us in.

After Mama-Annie had told her all she knew, Grandma Julia turned to me and asked, "And the boy won't marry you?"

"I'd not have him if he would!" I said.

"I see," she said with great dignity. She was in her mid-seventies then, and was small and thin and quick like a bird. She turned to Mama-Annie.

"I believe I will be traveling to New York one last time before I...," she paused, "...retire. I will, of course, require a traveling companion and I can think of no one better suited than Julia. Since John Forbes allowed Doreen to travel to Richmond for her education, he surely won't refuse his own mother's request to have Julia accompany me. Tell him I promise that she too will be educated." Mama-Annie nodded. Grandma Julia then turned to me. "You do want to go, do you not?"

I nodded. What other choice was there?

"Then you're to be here a week from Friday, and we'll leave the following day," she said to me. "It will take me a few days to make arrangements for our accommodations." Then to Mama-Annie again, "You've not told John Forbes anything?"

Mama-Annie shook her head. "He don't suspect," she replied.

"Good!" said Grandma Julia. "I expect the news would kill him. Or at least break his heart. Tell him only what I've told you, so this trip seems like my idea. He surely won't begrudge an old lady one last fling."

I smiled through my shame. She went to a little table, opened a drawer, took out some money which she counted out bill by bill, and then pressed into my hand.

"This is for your train ticket to come here next week," she said. "It would be less complicated for you to come here. My yard-man will meet you at the station next Saturday. Now, don't worry about packing very much. We shall get all you need in New York."

She invited us to sit down a while and visit, but Mama-Annie politely declined. We had a good fifteen mile trip ahead of us, and Mama-Annie never liked to stay away from her home for very long. She did allow the boys to get out of the buggy and accept some lemonade. While Johnny and Willie drank their lemonade on the porch, Grandma Julia told Mama-Annie,

"Thank you Annie-Pearl for coming to me about this situation. I do appreciate your trust." To me, she added, "Do you realize, Julia, that Annie Pearl was the same age you are now when she married your Papa?"

I'd never thought of Mama-Annie young. She'd seemed like a grown woman when she came to our house to raise us and be Papa's wife. I couldn't imagine her young, yet she was far from old.

Papa took the news of my travel with Grandma Julia quite well and didn't suspect a thing. When he drove me to the depot and put me on the train for Rocky Mount, he said good-by as if I'd only be gone a few weeks.

Grandma Julia had made all the plans. As our train steamed northward, I sat back in my seat and admired the lovely October landscape and wondered what life had in store for me. We stopped in Philadelphia for a few days—such a big, bustling city, so many people—that I was overwhelmed.

"Wait until you see New York, my dear," said Grandma Julia.

She was right. New York was more than I could ever have imagined. Grandma Julia had found us wonderful lodging on Park Avenue. A friend of hers who was touring Europe for a year had graciously lent it to her. For the first few days, I wandered around the apartment, marveling that any human could live in a place so grand.

When we went out, as we did every day, I saw buildings so high I could barely see the tops. Grand ladies carrying parcels went in and out of more stores than I could ever shop in. Everyone was hurrying somewhere so fast. There was talk the war might end soon, and everyone was excited about it. All the activity made my head spin.

One evening when we came in, I felt sick. I must have overdone it, I thought, trying to see so much so fast. Besides my dizziness, my throat was scratchy and every bone in my body seemed to ache. Grandma Julia sent for a doctor, who put me straight to bed. I had influenza, he said. There was a great deal of it going around. I was to rest and drink plenty of liquids. I remember that much. Then there was a long stretch of time when I didn't remember anything.

I remember a sensation of falling through darkness, and hands pulling at my body—first one way and then another, and voices in the darkness—voices I couldn't quite make out, and strange dark dreams. Or were they dreams? Once from out of the darkness an angel appeared and stared at me, her nose almost against mine. She said to me, "Live! Live!" A beautiful angel with red-gold hair and the sweetest voice I've ever heard, she appeared again and again, and each time after the first, she said, "Not yet!" and drew further away, until she was a tiny, tiny little speck in the darkness.

One morning I awoke and thought the angel stood beside my bed, but this time she was in silhouette with the morning sun streaming in the window behind her. I couldn't make out her features, but I knew by her presence she was both beautiful and terrible. Her voice was demanding, not sweet. She grasped my hand, and I heard her say, "You will live, Julia! You will live!" and I knew it was Grandma Julia and not an angel who spoke to me.

"Grandma Julia?" I said. "Am I dead?"

"No, child," she answered. "You're here with me."

"The baby?" I asked, suddenly remembering.

She didn't reply. A man came forward from the corner of the room. He must have been the doctor.

"I'm sorry," he said, "I did what I could. But you were very ill...." his voice trailed off. It wasn't until much later that he told me I'd probably never be able to have children. I should be happy, I thought, now everything's back the way it was. That wasn't so. Nothing would ever again be the way it was. Never in your life can you take back what's happened.

From that day, my body grew stronger but my spirit sagged. Grandma Julia tried her best to interest me in things. She played all the pieces of music I knew and some I didn't. She read to me—history and geography and mythology and the Bible. Nothing interested me.

Finally she said, "You're not going to sit around and feel sorry for yourself! I won't allow it! You're going to come out of this better and smarter and with more knowledge and wisdom than you ever thought possible," she insisted. "Did I ever tell you about when I was at Chimborazo Hospital during the War? I saw boys die. I held some by the hand while doctors sawed off their legs. And screaming? You never heard such screaming! Those that survived were glad to sacrifice an arm or leg if it meant saving their lives. You have a family that loves you. It would break you father's heart if he lost you. It would break mine. The loss you suffered wasn't any greater than what thousands of other women haven't already suffered. And you're far luckier than most. Look."

She thrust the newspaper in front of me. I read about the influenza epidemic raging the country that had claimed thousands of lives—sometimes whole families. I realized that I was fortunate. I vowed that I'd live again.

Grandma Julia wrote to Mama-Annie and Papa, telling them about the influenza and that, given my weakened condition, I would not be returning home until I regained my strength. She did not mention my losing the baby, but I felt like Mama-Annie somehow knew. While I recuperated, Grandma Julia taught me history and French, and read me books she'd always liked, and—of course—taught me more music. As I grew stronger, she took me to museums and theaters and music halls. At first I was reluctant to go out, but before long I went gladly, then eagerly.

When Mama-Annie wrote back, enclosing a small clipping from the county paper that reported the death from influenza at boot camp of a young soldier, Eben Hubbler, I felt no particular emotion. He'd never be a hero, not now, not ever. A chapter in a book had been closed, never to be read again, but the rest of the book lay open before me. I was eager for the knowledge—for whatever Grandma Julia wanted me to learn.

One day, as we sat at the piano, I asked Grandma Julia about my mother.

"Why doesn't Papa ever speak of her?" I wondered.

"He had loved her too much," she replied. "If he talked about her, the way she was in the past, he'd have to think about her death all over again. It was easier for him to never speak of her again. I thought he'd never get over it. But he had the horses—the horses they both loved. The horses were his saving grace. And he had you and Doreen."

Then she told me all about my mother—how beautiful she was, and how she could sing and play, and how she loved life.

"Your Grandmother Cabell took the wrong one back to Richmond with her," Grandma Julia admitted. "She wanted her daughter back. Doreen might have had Dorie's hair, but you have her talent and her soul. Isn't it odd how people can be so deceived by appearances?"

She changed the subject without seeming to change it. "Here's a Mozart sonata Dorie especially liked," Grandma Julia said. Her fingers flew over the keyboard.

I spent the rest of the day learning that sonata, and even now I can sit down at a piano and play it all the way through without looking at the music.

When all my strength had returned, Grandma Julia took me with her as she visited old friends of hers. I noticed that her voice was different when she spoke to people in New York. She sounded like them. People in New York talked so different, not easy and soft and slow like people back home, but hard and sharp. It put me in mind of a butcher knife, the way a northern person's voice had an edge to it. They talked so fast, how did they ever have time to think about what they wanted to say?

When I asked Grandma Julia about it, she said, "When in Rome, child, you do as the Romans do."

I was puzzled.

"It means," she said, "you must act like the people around you. It makes them feel more comfortable if you're not so different from them. It's good manners."

"Oh," I said, and after that I tried harder to talk like them. Grandma Julia made suggestions: if I said, "Won't it nice?" she corrected me and made me repeat back,"Wasn't it nice?" She made me say the *g*'s on the ends of my words, which made the words sit hard against my teeth. She stopped me from saying "aiming to" or "fixing to."

"People here," explained Grandma Julia, "just do what they intend. They aren't *aiming* to do it or *fixing* to do it. They just *do* it!"

She corrected me in other ways, too. If I tucked my napkin into the neck of my dress to keep my dress nice instead of putting it on my lap, Grandma Julia would say, "When in Rome, Child, when in Rome," and I would know to copy what she was doing.

She often played piano for the friends she visited, and before long was introducing me as her protege. I was nervous the first time I played, but soon began to enjoy the attention. As my repertoire and skill increased, I looked forward to performing. When President Wilson announced the end of the war, it seemed that everyone in New York held a party to celebrate, and we went to most of them. One evening, after playing at an especially elegant supper party, I looked up from the keyboard into the bluest eyes I'd ever seen. That's how I met Benjamin Tartleton Harrington, Jr., and the rest, as they say, is history.

He'd lately returned from France, he said, and still had on his lieutenant's uniform. His father, a prominent industrialist, held this party to celebrate his safe return. He'd not feel he'd returned safely, he confided, until he danced with me. Almost on cue, a small orchestra stuck up the notes of a Strauss waltz, and Tarlie—for that was what I was to call him—led me onto the floor and whirled me around. From that moment, my heart was his.

Ours was a story-book romance. We saw each other daily all that winter. We went everywhere in New York there was to go. Whenever I accepted an invitation to play for an event, Tarlie was in the audience. On a wintry day in 1919, when the sky spat snow but the air promised spring, we took a carriage ride through Central Park, and Tarlie asked me to marry him and I accepted. His father arranged for the wedding to be held in mid-September in his townhouse with the reception following at the Waldorf.

I wrote Papa and Mamma-Annie the news, begging them to come, but they declined. Mama-Annie didn't like to travel far from home; Papa was too busy with the tobacco; my little brothers were too rambunctious to travel all that way on the train. They hoped I understood and sent their best wishes. Tarlie and his parents and Grandma Julia and I went back to Penhook for a visit that summer. Both families seemed to hit it off, but

Patches on the Same Quilt

Mama-Annie, even though she liked Tarlie well enough, took me aside to tell me her worries.

"What kind of a name is Harrington, anyway?" she wanted to know. "Who's his people? What if one of his kin-folks was the Yankee who shot your Great-uncle John?"

Mama-Annie worries about everything.

Grandmother Cabell and Doreen came in from Richmond to look over the prospective in-laws. Though Grandmother Cabell was distressed that I was marrying a Yankee, she was delighted that I was marrying well. She was very much in her element, comparing notes with Tarlie's mother about long-ago ancestors and politely not mentioning the immediate ones who might have faced each other in battle. Doreen was quiet and lady-like and didn't say much. She was nothing at all like the older sister I remembered. Nonetheless, she was my sister—the only one I had—so I asked her to be in the wedding party as my maid of honor. Grandmother Cabell accepted for her without hesitation, even though it meant that Doreen would have to miss a week of college.

My wedding ceremony was all that I hoped it would be. Though I missed having Papa and Mama-Annie with me, Grandma Julia was at least there to play my wedding music. At the reception, Grandmother Cabell fawned over me as if I had been her chosen one. Discreetly—but not discreetly enough to keep Doreen from blushing beet-red, she inquired of the Harringtons if they had any more eligible young men in the family. Her hopes dashed by their negative reply, she circulated among the large crowd of guests, with Doreen in tow behind her, as she searched for prospects. As Tarlie and I danced together, he whispered in my ear that he'd bet she'd searched through all the eligible Richmond families already and had only accepted our invitation because it opened up previously uncharted territories for her. I laughed in agreement, and silently promised myself that I'd never again envy Doreen.

Grandma Julia surprised us all by announcing her return to Virginia. Her mission, she said, had been accomplished. "I know you'll be in good hands," she said as she winked at Tarlie. Her wedding present to us was a written-out itinerary of a trip to Greece and Rome and the cash to make it possible.

"This is the same route that Charles and I followed on our first trip abroad together. I want you to see the old things through young eyes," she said.

However, she advised us to wait until the international situation had settled before we ventured across the ocean. We had so much to do, moving into the townhouse that Tarlie's father had given us, that we agreed to take her advice. Satisfied that we were pleased with her gift, she resumed her seat at the piano and played the Mozart sonata that I loved so much.

Several months later, when Tarlie and I returned to our hotel from a day-long jaunt about the seven hills of Rome, there was a telegram waiting for us. It was from Papa.

"Your grandmother has suffered a stroke," it said. "If you want to see her alive, you need to come home." The rest of the words swam before my eyes.

Tarlie booked passage immediately while I packed. Ten days later, we were in Virginia. Grandma Julia was still alive, but barely. She couldn't speak and could barely move. Her eyes lit up when I walked into her room. I know she knew me. She seemed to listen when I told her about how wonderful our trip had been—just like she promised it would be.

I ws describing the wonders of Italy when her nurse came in and told us we'd better go—"Miz Julia needs her rest now. You come on back tomorrow."

I took Grandma Julia's hand and told her, "Thank you for my life."

Those were the last words I spoke to her. She died early the next morning.

At her funeral, I was the one who played the piano for her. She'd left instructions that her funeral was not to be a sad occasion, but rather a celebration of her life.

"I've done far more than I ever dreamed I'd do, and gone to places I never dreamed I'd visit," she wrote in a letter to be read at her service. "Do not be sad that my life is over. I've seen my every wish come true, and I've lived life to the fullest. What more is there for me to do on earth?"

She'd left a list of music she wanted me to play. The last one was the Mozart piece. Papa left the room when I started to play it. Was he mourning his mother, I wondered, or his first wife?

After Grandma Julia had been buried in the family graveyard on the hill, the neighbors crowded around to pay their respects and to meet Tarlie. So many people spoke to me in the familiar speech that had been such a part of me. I found myself slipping back into the soft tones of the central Virginia accent.

"Ain't it a mess of folks up in New York?" a neighbor asked me. "How do y'all keep from gittin' lost?"

"It won't hard to find my way around," I told her, "once I figgered where I was aimin' to go."

"Your husband seems like a right nice boy," she said, looking in his direction as he smiled back at her from a a short distance away, "but, I declare, he talks so funny I cain't make out half what he says."

Tarlie had overheard the conversation.

"I talk funny?" he said that evening as we walked down to the barn to look at the horses. "I? The people down here are the ones who talk in such a peculiar manner. And, Julia, it surprises me that you've begun to talk just like them!"

I looked into his eyes and smiled my most charming smile.

"When in Rome, my dear," I said, "When in Rome...."

Chapter 10
WILLIE WEBSTER

TAKING UP THE REINS

Livin' your life, my daddy said, is not unlike ridin' a horse. To be any good at it, you got to know when to ride easy and when to take up the reins, when to let the horse make the decisions and when to take control. I'm a plenty good rider. I rode and showed my daddy's horses all over Virginia—into North Carolina, Kentucky, and Tennessee, too. Wherever there was a fair or a big horse show, we'd go.

I had the kind of boyhood that some kids only dream about. As soon as I was big enough to walk, my daddy had me on a horse. Even before that, he'd set me in the saddle in front of him and put my hands on the reins and play like I was controllin' the horse. 'Course, his hands were always over top of mine.

My daddy raised fine horses—still does, to some extent—but people don't want horses much anymore. There's so many faster ways to get where you want to go. But my daddy loves a horse. Always had, he told me, always will.

"There's a rhythm to life," he once said, "something like the rhythm a singlefootin' horse makes. You can hear that rhythm beatin' in your ear, feel it all through your whole body. Seems like it plays a tune."

I never thought much about it then, but lately, it strikes me he was right. Trouble is, I want my life to move a lot faster than the natural rhythm of life here on the farm.

I remember, way back when I won't more than eight or nine, Daddy had me ride horses for his customers. "So gentle a child can handle them," he liked to brag. And I showed them, too in all those places we went, travelin' all day and sometimes all night by boxcar. We always rode the boxcar with the horses. Daddy'd never trust them to anybody else. Other horse people rode in the coaches and sat in fine plush seats and looked out the window at the world goin' by and ate dinner in the dinin' car and left their horses to the grooms, but we sat on bales of hay and ate a box dinner that Mama'd fixed.

"If a box-car's good enough for the finest horses in the state of Virginia," Daddy'd always say when I complained, "I reckon it's good enough for us. 'Sides," he'd wink, "no train cook can out-do your mama when it comes to fixin' fried chicken."

I reckon he was right. I didn't have any reason to complain. Sometimes, though, I think ridin' them trains is what ruined me. The trains went so fast it seemed like they set the rhythm of my life for me. They went faster than any horse could ever go, and their wheels clacked out *"Gotta-go-gotta-go-gotta-go"* over and over 'til it stuck in my head and I could never be satisfied with anything slower again.

'Course I always liked to go fast. When I was a kid, I used to race mules without Daddy knowin' about it. Well, eventually he found out about it, but I'd been racin' for a spell by then. A bunch of us kids used to get together on Sundays down by the Pigg River and run our daddies' work mules. I don't remember exactly how we got started, but it got to be a regular Sunday afternoon thing. After church, our daddies would sit around and rest up after dinner, so we knowed they wouldn't need the mules. We'd each of us get a mule from our barn-lot and slip off down to the river where we'd meet and organize the race. At first, we raced for fun, but then we started putting up a little money. I always rode Ranger, a big-boned, red gaited mule who could rack almost as fast as he could gallop. He was Daddy's best mule, but he was barn-sour. It helped considerable that the finish line was in the direction of home, though Ranger about pulled my arms outta their sockets when I tried to stop him once we won, which we usually did.

It won't hard to sneak Ranger off either. I'd lead him in a straight line with the barn until we came to the tobacco field. Along side the field was a drop-off, so we wouldn't be seen from the house if the tobacco was high enough. I'd hop on Ranger's back there—I rode bareback; we all did. No use leavin' tell-tale sweat marks on a saddle. Daddy always cleaned his saddles and bridles of a Saturday. Fresh white sweat marks and a wet saddle would be a dead give-away that I'd not risk. I'd pieced together a racin' bridle out of odds and ends of rope. I dared not risk borrowin' one of Daddy's polished bits, so I ran a piece of rope through Ranger's mouth and reined him with that—kinda like the Indians did, I reckon.

On that day, the last day I raced, I had a time slippin' off. Seemed like Mama kept findin' chores for me to do. Finally, she took up my baby sister Hannah and went to set in a rocker on the front porch. I hurried out to get Ranger as fast as I could go. The Pigg River was a great racin' place. You didn't get hurt bad if you fell off onto the flat sandy strip of bank, and you could wash the sweat off the mules in the river after the race. When Ranger and me got to the riverbank, they was a bunch ready to go and a crowd to watch.

"We about give up on you," said Amos Ratley, the unofficial organizer. "How much you got?"

"Five cents," I told him.

"Pitch her in thar," he said, opening a square of sackin' and then tyin' it back up when I pitched in my money.

I looked around to see who else was runnin'. Little Rufe Hubbler was straddlin' a mule so skinny he might have been ridin' a fence rail.

There was two Muse brothers I didn't know real well from down below Peckerwood Level. I'd seen 'em around, though. They rode matchin' white mules, their daddy's buggy team, I reckon. One of the boys wore a set of big ol' spurs. The last rider was a girl—that dark-headed little Patty Cundiff on a big, long-legged black mule.

"We ain't never had a gal race before," I said.

"Let her ride," said Amos. "She pitched in more'n twice what you did."

"You're just afraid I'll whip you!" she said. "And I will, too. You're just scared you're gonna get beat by a girl!"

I didn't say nothin', but turned Ranger toward a black willow tree and pulled me off a long switch, just in case. I skinned off the leaves as we rode down to the startin' line, about a quarter mile away, where Amos had taken a stick and scratched a mark into the sand. While we lined up, Amos shinnied up the tree and hung the prize money from a limb. The winner would be the one to grab the money. You had to grab it by the top. If you was to grab the bottom, all the money'd fall out and the kids watchin' would nigh about stomp each other racin' to get it.

Amos waited until all the watchers had made their side bets. Then he yelled, "One-two-three-*GO*!"

All the mules lunged forward, most of them knowin' that the sooner we got this business over with, the sooner they could go home. Mules is smart like that.

The Muse boy wearin' spurs must've dug them into his mule's side because his mule spurted forward, then stopped dead, and bucked hard enough to pitch the boy into the river. The other white mule stopped when his buddy did. That left three of us still runnin', but the Hubbler mule was heavey, and I could hear him breathin' hard and coughin'. I knew he'd dropped back when I couldn't hear him any more.

That gal on the black mule stayed neck and neck with Ranger and me. Her fingers was laced into the mane, and she crouched low on his neck. Her legs hammered so loud against his sides I could hear them over the sound of the hoofbeats. Both mules was sweatin' to beat the band. It was all we could do to keep from slidin' off. I could hear the watchers yellin' and cheerin'. I raised my switch and whopped it as hard as I could on Ranger's rump. He edged ahead of the black mule, and I now held on to his mane with my switch hand while I let go of the reins with my other hand so I could get the money. I stretched up, grabbed for it, and got it! The prize was mine! That little gal was madder'n a wet hen.

I tried to pick up the reins and stop Ranger so everybody could congratulate me, but Ranger was already home-ward bound. When I finally got the reins back, I pulled as hard as I could, and the rope bit broke. I reckon Ranger'd chewed through it. He lunged forward and ran flat out—faster even than he ran in the race. Won't nothin' to do but hang onto his mane as best I could and keep my mind on not lettin' go of my prize money. I should've been scared, but I won't. This was the fastest I'd ever gone in my life—except for the train—and it was like flyin'. I figgered won't nothin' to do but enjoy it while it lasted.

Ranger didn't exactly follow the same route goin' as he did comin'. He took considerable short-cuts. I bit my lip and tasted blood when he rared back and jumped Polecat Creek. I got scratched up a mite when he went through some scrub pines. I didn't care—that mule could flat fly! I knew there won't no stoppin' him so I started to consider where I could jump off him before he got home and took me through the low door into his stall. I decided the best place to jump off was just after we went around the tobacco patch. The ground was as soft there as it would ever be.

This plan would've worked except, instead of runnin' around the tobacco patch, Ranger went dead through the middle of it, takin' out the better part of a row without so much as breakin' stride. I confess I was lookin' down at the time and wonderin' how I'd explain it. If I'd been lookin' up, I'da seen Mama standin' there. About that time, Ranger cleared the tobacco patch, I fell off and landed right smack at Mama's feet. Mama grabbed what was left of the willow switch I was still clutchin' and lit into me, not stoppin' until the switch was wore down to a twig.

Then she lit into me with her tongue, sayin', "Gamblin' on a Sunday! Ain't you ashamed! Shamin' us all! Runnin' that poor mule on his one day of rest!"

She said lots more, but that was the gist of it. She snatched up the prize money and put it in her apron pocket, vowing that it was goin' in the collection plate at church next Sunday. Then she told me I'd best forget about supper and go right straight to bed as soon as I curried the sweat off Ranger. I truly believe that was the maddest I ever seen Mama get. Usually she was a woman of few words who kept her temper to herself.

Daddy—who I know for a fact was sittin' in the side yard under the big maple tree—couldn't help but of heard Mama, but he didn't come around the house to save me. I felt a mite bad about it, until he slipped up to my room after supper with a chicken leg and a piece of apple pie.

While I ate, he told me, "You ought not've done it, but long as you did, I'm mighty proud you won." He shook my hand and winked and said, "But don't tell your mama or your brother I said so."

I thought about that race for a long time after—not the race exactly, but the feelin's I had—flyin' and free and both scared and thrilled at the same time—like I was the only one in the world who'd ever felt feelin's like that. I know my brother Johnny never felt like that. Johnny is not like me. He's a worker like Mama. Mama's always up before daylight ever' day. She fixes us a big breakfast, cleans up, fixes dinner, cleans up, fixes supper, and cleans up. She never sets down to eat—just hovers over us, makin' sure we got enough. I don't recollect she ever sets down except at church and whenever there's something to be done—like sewin' or snappin' beans—that requires settin' to do it. Johnny must've took after her—he's always busy. He's always tendin' the stock—when he was just a kid, he bought his first calves from money he saved doin' odd jobs for neighbors. Few years later he had a whole herd. Same with tobacco—had hisself a little extry patch when he was younger, and every year since he makes a bigger patch. Anything that'll turn to money, he'll raise. But the rhythm of his life is a slow rhythm—the plodding kind of rhythm you have when you follow behind a plow all day.

Daddy works, too, but with him it's different. Daddy is a dreamer. I guess I take after him. Mama and Johnny are always lookin' down at what they're doin'—the seam she's sewin' or the furrow he's plowin'. Daddy is always lookin' up. Up and out. Long time ago, I asked him what he was lookin' at, and he told me he was lookin' at the far horizon. When I was a kid, I tried to see it, but all I saw was tree-tops. I see the horizon now. I see you got to ride your life just like you'd ride a horse.

When Daddy taught me to ride, he said, "Always keep your eyes lookin' in the distance to see what's comin'. The horse'll take care of lookin' at what's right in front. Look right between his ears and over his head. You drop your head, the horse will slow down and shuffle along lazy. You want to show a horse, you sit tall and proud, and that horse'll just naturally step out tall and proud hisself."

I rode plenty of horses for Daddy when he was sellin' 'em. He'd stand beside a customer and talk quiet and polite—maybe ask the man about his family or the weather—while I rode that horse around and around just as easy. The man would see how fine the horse was—why, a little boy could ride him! Daddy'd get his price. That was Daddy's work and Daddy's dream, too—to raise and sell fine horses.

The horse shows were really somethin', though. Sometimes in Tennessee—usually Shelbyville or Wartrace or maybe Murfreesboro—there might be twenty or thirty horses in a class. I'd most always come out with a ribbon, and plenty of times that ribbon was blue. People I didn't even know would holler for me when I took my victory pass, and they'd crowd around me and pat me on the back when I dismounted. A fellow gets used to attention like that real easy, and when there ain't no people cheerin', you tend to feel a mite slighted.

Now Johnny couldn't be like that. If anyone was to ever cheer for him, he'd turn red as a beet and hide his face. He never liked the show ring and the crowds. Daddy taught him to ride same as me, but Johnny's heart won't in it. One time, he fell off and then got his foot stomped on when he tried to remount. That done it. He never again wanted no part of ridin'. To this day, he still limps from that foot-stompin', but it satisfies him just fine to be behind the plow that a horse or mule pulls, limp or no limp.

Farmin's in Johnny's blood, but not in mine. You can't go no place when you farm. You're tied to your land, is how I see it. Farmer's always got his feet in the dirt. I gotta go places. Sometimes I lay awake nights and dream of places to go.

One time when I was about twelve years old, while we were ridin' a box-car bound for somewhere far away, Daddy told me about when he was about my age—how he dreamed so bad about havin' a horse and how his dream came true. He told me about dreamin' of meetin' the prettiest gal that ever was, and that dream came true, too. Trouble with dreams, he said, is they don't last. You always got to keep dreamin' new ones.

I asked him if he dreamed about marryin' Mama, and he told me no. "Sometimes you got to step out of your dream," he said, "and be practical. Sometimes what's for the best ain't part of a dream."

He was quiet for a minute, like he was thinking about something long ago and far away. The only sounds around us in the dark of the box-car was the horses breathin' soft and the train wheels sayin' "*gotta-go-gotta-go.*" Finally he spoke again.

"Son," he said, "there's always two ways to go in life. You can go toward somethin' or you can go away from somethin'. Most of my life was spent movin' toward somethin'—at least until my first wife died. Seemed like a fog came over me then, and I couldn't see which way to go. The reins slipped through my fingers and I couldn't find them. But I kept goin' through the motions of livin'. My mama told me, 'You've got children. You've got to go on for them.' So I kept movin', but I didn't know where. That fog stayed on me for a couple of years—I married your mama durin' that time. I hardly knew her, but I knew she was a good woman. I regret to say I didn't treat her as good as she deserved. I'd go for days at a time in those days and barely talk to her. It won't her fault. She was as fine a woman as a man would want—better than I deserved at the time. But she won't Dorie. I kept waitin' for Dorie, thinkin' she'd come back, knowin' there won't no way. All that time, I was movin' away from my life. It won't 'til the day you were born that I started movin' back."

Then he told me about the day I was born.

"I recollect just as plain," he said, "I was sittin' by the fireplace in the front room mindin' little Johnny while Granny Odell and her girl Rose-Ella were upstairs with your mama. Your sisters were at school. Julia had just started that year. Seems like I was still dreamin'—all I could think of was my first wife and how she died havin' the little boy that died, too—a few months after. Johnny was toddlin' around, the way babies will. I was supposed to be watchin' him, but I won't half payin' attention. It was a cold day. There was a fire in the fireplace, but I kept lookin' out that little window, up toward the graveyard. I didn't see little Johnny headin' toward the fire. Then, all of a sudden, you were born—I heard you cry out just as loud—and the fog lifted like somethin' jerked me back to my senses, I grabbed Johnny just before he tumbled into the fire. After that, it seems like I started goin' toward somethin' again—like I picked up the reins again. My life started again the day you were born. I started treatin' your mama better, for one thing."

I didn't know what to say to him. Seemed like that wasn't the kind of thing a daddy ought to tell his child. After he told me that, I couldn't tell him my dreams of goin' far away and livin' fast. Daddy wants me to take up with the horses when he leaves off. He don't understand that horses is on their way out. Already more cars are on the roads than horses. Soon won't nobody want nor need a horse. You can't tell Daddy, though.

Well, I know he thinks I'm movin' away from things. The last few years, I've moved away from home more times than I can count. I go off somewhere and get a job for a while, then I move away from it and come back home. Every time, Daddy thinks I'm back to stay. Before long, I leave again, I see disappointment wrote all over his face, but I'm movin' toward somethin'. I just don't know what.

For a spell, I worked in the mines in West Virginia. Soon as I got my paycheck, I left. I couldn't stand to be down in the dark all day. Went to Roanoke for a while and worked odd jobs. Learned a little about automobile mechanics. Now that's a job with a future. People always gonna need cars fixed. Cars always gonna break down. But it's a slow job. You're stuck in a garage all day. Went out to Woodrum Flyin' Field and watched planes land and take off. Met a man who'll teach me to fly a plane if I can scrape up a little money. That's the comin' thing—airplanes! Won't be long 'til ever'body'll have one. People flyin' all over the place—anywhere they want to go!

That's what I dream of doin'—flyin' way up in the clouds—faster than a horse or a car can go—way over the far horizon.

Becky Mushko

Chapter 11
HANNAH WEBSTER

ONE TINY SPECK OF TRUTH

People are all the time saying how smart I am. Most times they say, "Hannah is so smart, but—" and they throw in something like "Hannah just doesn't use her God-given talents" or some such as that.

Now this is not exactly true, if you ask me. I do so use my God-given talents. The only thing is that no one else appreciates them but me. For one thing, I have a very good imagination. I like to make up stories to entertain myself because I am the only young one in my family. The others are either old or dead. For instance, my mama died this past year, and my daddy is an old gray-headed man. The few live ones—mainly my grown-up brothers Johnny and Willie—are usually too busy to talk to me, or if they ain't busy, they're too tired. Lots of times when I crave company, I go up to the graveyard on the hill and talk to the ones up there. I hope they hear me. Trouble is, they never do answer me back.

For another thing, it is true that I am very smart. I have won several spelling medals. I can read faster than anyone in the sixth grade and faster than most of the seventh grade too. I come by my smartness naturally. My daddy went to college and his daddy even taught college. My daddy's mama taught something, too. Piano, I believe it was. My mama's people never went to school much, but they were naturally smart and didn't need much schooling. That's the way I figure it.

My sister Doreen is very smart. She's an old maid school teacher. She doesn't like to be called that. Plus she's not exactly my sister—she is a half-sister, even though she is a whole person but very short. I am taller right now than she is. She explained to me that we are half-sisters because we had different mamas but the same daddy. Her mama was Daddy's first wife. She died a long, long time ago. My sister Julia is my half-sister for the same reason. My brothers are all my own.

Doreen has got this notion that I should call her "Aunt" Doreen now that I live with her on account she thinks it is embarrassing for there to be so much difference in our ages. I cannot help that.

Doreen brought me to live with her a few months after Mama died because Daddy is such an old man and it wasn't proper for me to grow up running wild—as Doreen said, but that is not my opinion—with only Daddy and my two grown brothers to look after me. I tried to explain to her that it was the other way around—that I was the one who looked after them and cooked and cleaned and did the washing and everything just fine, thank you—but Doreen is one of these people who does not want to be told what is contrary to her own beliefs. She just said, "That proves my point!"

"But they need me on the farm!" I told her. "I don't want to leave the farm!"

"That's another thing," she said. "Doing farm work like a field hand! Riding bareback! No proper supervision! Whatever must Papa be thinking?"

To make a long story short, that is how I came to live in Richmond and go to the school where she is an old maid school teacher and where, as Doreen says, she can "keep an eye on me." Everyone—other teachers, that is—tell me how lucky I am to have "Aunt" Doreen to look after me and raise me proper. I think I was luckier before. Before Mama died of a busted appendix and before "Aunt" Doreen decided I was in need of civilizing, I did just fine.

As soon as Mama was covered up and we was all making our way down the graveyard hill, Doreen came alongside of me and patted my shoulder and said, "I know what it is to lose a mother. Fortunately, when I was just a mere child, your mother was there to look after me. I shall do the same for you, since I truly doubt that Papa will ever marry again at his age."

I didn't say anything then, so Doreen just thought I was overcome with grief and let me alone for a while.

Almost every day, I think back to that cold blue day last March when we had Mama's funeral up on the hill in the family graveyard. It was a home funeral. Everybody including the preacher came to our house. Some of Mama's people had made her a casket. Her sisters who are my real aunts—not like Doreen—washed her and dressed her and fixed her hair and put her in the casket. She laid in her casket in the front room like she was sleeping peaceful and not hurting anymore while we waited for everyone to get there.

Mama knew for about a week that she was going to die, and she didn't hold with doctors so we didn't get one until it was too late for him to do anything except tell that Mama had appendicitis and her appendix had probably busted. I already accepted the fact that she would die because she had called me to her and said it was God's Will that her time had come and that it would be my job to be a good girl and look after Daddy and do what I was told. I don't think she had it in mind that I would be told by Doreen. I don't even think that Doreen figured into God's Will, neither.

Mama was buried one space over from Doreen's mama. Daddy told me that the space between was for him when his time came, and would I see to it that his wish was respected. I promised I would. That way he could be buried beside both his wives. Maybe that was why Doreen said he'd never marry again—there ain't a place for another one. When I asked Daddy where my place would be, he said not to think about that yet. My life, he said, was just getting started.

Our grave-yard is plumb full of kin folk. My grandmother and my great-grandparents who died before I was born and my Great-uncle John who was in the War are in the row behind, and my Daddy's great-grandparents and their kin are in the next row behind that. On the other side of Doreen's mama is a little tiny grave up against the iron fence. Daddy once told me that my little brother was buried there. On his grave, there's a little stone lamb that Doreen had bought in Richmond a few years ago and put there. I like that lamb. Sometimes I sit up there on my little brother's grave and pet his lamb while I talk to the people in the graveyard.

I asked Daddy about my little brother a long time ago.

"What was his name?" I wanted to know. "Who was he?"

"We never named him," Daddy told me.

I never asked him again and he never spoke of it again. From a little window beside the fireplace in our front room, I used to be able to see his grave. Then the pines and cedars grew too thick.

I said that everyone came to Mama's funeral, but this was not quite so. Julia didn't come. Or her husband neither. Julia is a very great lady who lives in New York and plays the piano for famous people. She is maybe the best piano player in the world. I think Julia must be something like a fairy princess, because her husband is handsome and rich just like in the stories that end happily ever after. They come to visit a few years ago, and she was the most beautiful lady I ever seen. Her husband is some kind of business man and he talks funny. Not funny exactly, but hard and fast like he's in a big hurry. Not like people around here who have all the time in the world they want to say what they've a mind to. He's real skittish, too, like an unbroke colt. They was in Paris, France, when Mama died. Julia didn't get word until two weeks after, and she wrote Daddy a long letter saying how sorry she was. I wish she could have been here. Maybe she could have talked sense to Doreen.

Anyhow, at the funeral, I recollect that Doreen herself almost missed most of the service. She got there just as we was singing "Amazing Grace How Sweet The Sound." I recollect just as plain. She was huffing and puffing like a freight train and holding onto her hat because the wind was blowing pretty fair up on the hill. Her hat had a bunch of black feathers on it, and it put me in mind of a crow that wanted to fly off someplace on its own. Doreen said she was late because she had car trouble in Lynchburg. She had hopped in her car as soon as she got word, she said. Doreen is not real sensible, sometimes. She would likely have got here faster if she'd rode the train.

When we reached the bottom of the hill, Doreen started up on me again. She held onto her hat and told me again how my mama came to live with them when her mother died. She said how she could barely recollect her own mama now—only that she had reddish hair and sang a lot. But my mama had loved and raised her and Julia as if they was her own. At least raised her until Grandmother Cabell had come and took her to Richmond and gave her all the advantages. Doreen said she had been thinking about this all the way from Richmond, and that is why she decided to take me back with her—she owed my mama and Grandmother Cabell and this is how she could repay the debt. She was in a position to give me all the advantages, too.

I wish she had rode the train. If she had come by the train, she could have looked at the scenery and not thought so much and I would have been better off.

"What advantages?" I wanted to know.

"Well," Doreen said, "all sorts of things. Nice clothes. An education. Without an education, I would never have become a teacher."

I was not impressed. Being a teacher was not my idea of a good way to spend your life.

Before I could tell her how I felt about her chosen career, she said, "I believe it would honor the memory of your mother, my mother, and my grandmother if I took you to Richmond and gave you a proper up-bringing."

"I don't want to go," I told her. By then we was almost back at the house, and other people started up talking to us, so Doreen had to let me be.

That night, after Mama's kin-folks and the neighbors had finished visiting and eating up all the food everyone brought, and after Johnny and Willie had gone out to tend the stock, Doreen saw her chance to talk to Daddy about her plan. I slipped upstairs, but instead of going to bed, I sat on the top step so I could hear what they were saying without them seeing me. Even though I was bone-tired, I forced myself to stay awake so I could listen. They were on the settee in the front room. Doreen spoke so quiet, I couldn't hear what she said at first, but Daddy answered her loud.

"I've just lost her mother! Must I now lose her, too?" said Daddy, and I knew he meant me.

"Now, Papa, you know it's for the best," Doreen said. It sounded like she was trying extra hard to sound sweet. "You lost, as you put it, Julia and me, too. Look how well things turned out for us. Besides, you know you didn't really lose us."

She sounded too sweet to be true, now. Surely Daddy would catch on.

"Yes, I did," Daddy allowed. "Neither of you ever came back. At least not to stay. And when you did come back to visit, you weren't the same little girls I knew. You were different, changed. And sometimes I'm not sure it was for the best."

"Oh, Papa," Doreen said, "we grew up. You knew we had to grow up, didn't you?"

"Johnny and Willie grew up, too," Papa said, "but I still know them. They didn't change. Even when Willie takes one of his notions to go off somewhere, he still comes back the same and takes up where he left off."

I was getting too sleepy to follow along very well. I recollect they both had a few more things to say, but I forget just what. The back door opened, and Johnny and Willie come in, and Doreen decided she was too wore out to talk more. The last thing I heard was Daddy say to her, "I'll think on it." I hurried to get into bed before Doreen could climb the steps and catch me.

The next morning, Daddy broke it to me as easy as he could. He stroked my hair and he said it softly as if he was gentling a new colt and didn't want to startle it. As if he had to let it know that for all the strange new things it would go through, that things would be all right in the end. He hugged me close while I sobbed into his shoulder and finished up with, "...but you won't have to go 'til summer's over. You'll stay here with me 'til then."

Doreen looked fit to be tied when she saw that I wasn't going to go back with her right away, but she conceded the wisdom in letting me finish out the school year with my friends and then get used to the idea of going.

I wasn't quite as miserable as I thought I'd be. At least I had five months. Anything could happen in five months. Maybe

Doreen would meet a rich, handsome man and get married and live happily ever after like Julia and forget about me. Maybe she would decide to run off and join a circus or be an actress in the picture shows. Maybe....

While I waited for my life as I knew it to end—and wished for some momentous event to save me from my awful fate, I threw myself wholeheartedly into making the most of my summer. Every day, I rode my old pony Dollbaby as if each ride was my last. I ran through the fields, not caring if the chiggers ate me up—which they usually did, and waded deep into the creek, not caring if a snake bit me—which it didn't. I lived life with a vengeance, and savored every moment so it would stay in my mind forever and ever. I climbed the graveyard hill and told my miseries to all my people, and begged them to rise up and haunt Doreen just enough to scare her good so she'd let me be. I somehow knew they wouldn't. After all, Doreen was their family, too. Every week, a letter from Doreen arrived for me, and each week she described a new wonder that Richmond had to offer. The only ones that sounded the least bit interesting were the statues of Robert E. Lee and Stonewall Jackson on their horses on Monument Avenue. Maybe, I'd at least look at those when I got there.

Meanwhile, I tried to look at every little part of the farm—every last rock and tree and field and all the stock—but I couldn't look at everything hard enough, seemed like. Time passed too fast and ran through my fingers the way crawfish did when I tried to catch them in the creek.

The morning of the day I was supposed to get on the train and go to Richmond, Daddy hitched up his big bay gelding, Joyful Noise—we called him Noisy, for short—to the buggy and put my baggage under the seat. I thought it was awful early to leave, but then I had no idea how far it might be to Richmond. Daddy had put sleigh bells on Noisy's harness, so Noisy really was noisy. Daddy lifted me onto the seat and we started toward the Penhook depot, but Daddy passed it by and didn't stop the way I'd expected. In a few minutes we jingled past the Novelty depot, too, at a fast rack and headed for Union Hall. We didn't stop there neither. Just when I thought Daddy'd carry me all the way to Rocky Mount or maybe even Roanoke, he turned left onto the hard-packed clay road they call the old race path.

Daddy gave Noisy his head, and he racked so fast it felt like we was flying. Daddy put the reins in my hands and then reached his arms around me so his big worn hands covered my small ones, and we drove together—just like we was racing our buggy like boys used to do after church years ago. I know because my brother Willie used to do it.

Every so often, Daddy let go for a moment to point out who lived where as we passed. I guess so I wouldn't forget. He showed me the turn-off to the Smith cabin where he'd ridden Noisy's great-grandma when he went to ask my grampa if he could marry Mama. He told me that his Uncle John Forbes had racked Noisy's great-great-great-grandma on this very road eighty years ago, carrying a dipper of whiskey and not spilling a drop. I'd heard that story plenty of times. I'm glad he told it again.

Noisy crossed Houseman's Ford wide open, and water flew every which way. We both got wet. Daddy pointed out where the chestnut tree used to be that marked the finish point when he raced Noisy's great-great-grandma against a little horse not more than pony size—"In fact, she was old Dollbaby's great-great-grandma," he added, "ridden by the prettiest girl I'd ever in my life seen."

"Did you win?" I asked.

"It was a tie," he said. "No, come to think of it, I guess I did win. I won the best prize ever, but I lost something, too."

"What did you lose?" I wondered.

"My heart," he said. "I lost my heart."

I didn't understand what he meant, but I thought better than to ask him to explain, for his face took on an odd look, like he was looking into the distance and seeing something I couldn't see. Maybe wasn't meant to see.

We racked full tilt again until we pulled up at Bethel Church, and Daddy got out and tied Noisy to a tree. Noisy blew and shook hisself and jingled his bells. Daddy reached up and took my hand to help me down as if I was a great lady. He led me through the churchyard and pointed out old graves of people

Patches on the Same Quilt

who were kin to us. He showed me Preacher Martin's grave and told me he was some distant kin on the Smith side. He pointed to the place way off to the side of the woods where once—when he was about my age—he'd admired the most beautiful horse he'd ever seen, and he told me how the horse's owner had hoisted him up and given him a ride that he never forgot.

"Riding on that horse changed my life," he said. "After that ride, I was never quite the same person again that I'd been before."

He led me to the church step and told me to sit there while he went back to the buggy. I did, and he came back with a sack of biscuits and cold fried chicken and a quart jar of lemonade.

We sat and ate in silence and passed the jar of lemonade back and forth between us until it was empty. I wanted time to stop right then, but I knew it wouldn't. I did know that I would never forget this day and this buggy ride that Daddy had given me.

"I don't want to go to Richmond," I said.

"I don't want you to go, either," He said, "but we both know it's for the best. You need to be someplace your God-given talents can be developed. You need to see a little bit of the world beyond the farm."

I nodded, close to tears.

He went on, "Seems like every time a daughter of mine leaves, it about breaks my heart. Doreen wasn't too much older than you when her Grandma Cabell came and took her to Richmond to live. She gave Doreen all sorts of fine things that I could never give her. Why, Doreen would never have even been a teacher if Grandmother Cabell hadn't been there to see to her education.

"Now Julia was a bit older than you when her Grandma Webster needed her to go to New York as her traveling companion. Julia was a great comfort to her in her old age, and from her, Julia learned to play the piano. And Julia learned so much else. She's traveled all over—to Europe and everywhere. She met her husband in New York. If she'd stayed here, that never would have happened."

I nodded again. What he was saying was true, but it had been such a long time since I'd seen the lovely lady who was my sister Julia that it seemed she might have been someone I'd read about in a story instead of a real person.

He continued, "And I wasn't much older than you myself when I came to live on the farm. I missed my parents something terrible at first. But it's just like in the stories. You have to go off and seek your fortune before you can live happily ever after."

"Johnny didn't go off to seek his fortune, and he's living happily ever after," I pointed out. "He says he'll never leave the farm. And Willie keeps going off and coming back. He's never found his fortune no matter how many times he goes."

I expect that Willie will be going away again," Daddy said. "He's talking about joining the Air Force. And it is true that Johnny has stayed. But he understands that a farmer will never get rich. His heart's in farming, so he belongs here."

"Maybe my fortune's here, too" I allowed. "My heart's here. I could be a farmer."

Daddy laughed and thought for a minute.

"I tell you what," he said. "You go on and stay with Doreen a while. After you've been there a few years, you can decide for yourself what kind of a fortune you want to seek and where you want to be."

"I know now," I said, tears welling up in my eyes and spilling down my cheek. He reached up and brushed a tear off my face with his big callused thumb.

"You'll be back for Christmas," he said, "and for some time next summer. It won't be forever. Besides, you'll always be in my heart. Just like the penny in the tree. Do you recollect what I told you about the penny and the maple tree?"

"Yes," I said. "A long, long time ago, a big branch at the second fork of the old maple tree in the side yard broke off during a windy spell. You wanted to cut it off, but...your first wife...said, 'No, you can fix it back.' So you wired it together, but before you did, she put a penny inside the break. 'For good luck,' she said. You tied the branch to a higher branch so the wire would hold. Then the tree grew back together and the bark covered the wire and the tree still stands and the penny is still in there."

"Yes," he said, "the penny is still in there. After all these years. I can't see it, but I know it's there. And that branch still gives awful good shade. Hannah, I'll always hold you in my heart the way the tree holds the penny. And it breaks my heart—just like the tree limb broke—to let you go. But I'll piece it back together somehow and I'll always hold you deep inside it. Always."

He hugged me close. Then he led me to the buggy and lifted me in, untied Noisy, climbed in and picked up the reins, and drove off—not at a rack this time, at a walk so the bells were silent. A car chugged past us, breaking the silence and dusting Daddy and me. Noisy jumped a mite, then settled back into his walk.

"I remember when you'd never see a car on these roads," Daddy said. "Seems like you see one every time you go out nowadays. You couldn't pay me to have one. I'll take a horse over a car, any day."

When we came back to Union Hall depot, we'd made a complete big circle. A minute or two after we got there, the train pulled in, huffing and puffing and making Noisy snort.

Daddy spoke to the conductor for a minute and gave him a paper with directions to Doreen's house in case she wasn't there to meet me. He slipped some money into the conductor's hand, and the conductor promised to look out for me.

As the train pulled out, I pressed my face against the window and saw Daddy get back into his buggy and slap Noisy across the rump with the reins. Noisy took off, keeping pace with the train as he racked along the road that ran beside the tracks. They were still there beside the train when it stopped briefly at Novelty, and they were there again in Penhook. Only the glass window and a few feet of distance separated us. I thought might be Daddy was going to follow the train all the way to Richmond, but when the train pulled out from the Penhook depot, he turned Noisy toward home. A moment later, I lost sight of him, even though I pressed my face hard to the glass. I laid back in my seat and tried to sleep but couldn't. I felt all alone in a world that had suddenly become too big for me.

The trip seemed to take forever, but it was only a few hours before the train finally pulled into the Broad Street Station in Richmond. From my window. I saw Doreen's worried face studying each car in the train. I waved and caught her eye. She hustled me off as soon as the conductor handed me down my things. I almost had to run to keep up with her as her high heels clicked along to where she'd left her shiny black Ford.

Her car was so spotless clean that I was afraid I'd soil it with my travel dust. I hesitated, then got in.

After she put a key in a hole and turned it and worked some levers and pedals, we lurched off. As she drove, I looked at all the other cars on the road. I'd not ever seen so many all at once, and I was afraid they'd run into Doreen's car and kill us both. But somehow they didn't.

At one time, I might've thought it would be a grand thing to ride in a fine car like this, but now that I was actually doing it, I could see it didn't hold a candle to being in the buggy behind Noisy. I agreed with Daddy—I'd rather have a horse, any day.

It didn't take long to get to her house on a crowded street of other houses that looked like they stood shoulder to shoulder without much space in between. Each one had a little bitty patch of grass in front between the porch and the street. Hardly enough yard to sit in. You couldn't have put in a garden if you'd had a mind to. I wasn't much impressed with Richmond so far.

"We're home," Doreen said, but I knew this wasn't my home and never would be. I was right.

One of the first things "Aunt" Doreen did, after she'd moved me in and shown me off to the neighbors like I was some kind of prize livestock and got me enrolled in the school where she teaches, was to join me up for a literary club for young ladies that meets every other Tuesday afternoon in Miss Emily Wicklin's dark, high-ceilinged parlor. Miss Emily Wicklin is the assistant head-mistress at the school. I suspected "Aunt" Doreen wanted to impress her.

At these literary club meetings, mostly we sit there and sip tea out of little bitty cups and try not to look bored while Miss Emily Wicklin reads us poetry that is supposed to inspire us toward higher ideals in life. Some of the girls—"young ladies"—actually look interested sometimes, but in my opinion this sort of stuff can't hold a candle to riding bareback over the fields on a frosty day—which is what I'd be doing back home on the farm, but "Aunt" Doreen sets a considerable store by it. At first I refused to go to these silly meetings, but I learned quick enough that my life, though considerably duller and more miserable than what I'd been used to, could quite possibly get worse if I didn't give in to whatever notions "Aunt" Doreen had. That's how I figured out if I say, "My, that certainly is interesting!" every so often like I mean it, then Miss Emily Wicklin will think I am interested and won't expect much more of me, and neither will "Aunt" Doreen. It is easy to fool both of them.

Last week, Miss Wicklin was even more fluttery than usual, and normally she strikes me as a very fluttery person. She always puts me in mind of a high-strung horse, all wide-eyed and champing the bit.

"Young ladies," she said to settle us down, "I have a wonderful announcement. We shall have an essay contest, and the winner shall receive a five dollar gold piece and a lovely certificate. The subject of your essay is to be 'A Glimpse Into Family History.' It will be a marvelous opportunity for you to demonstrate both your writing skill and your knowledge of your heritage."

She smiled. Several of the prissier girls applauded.

One thing I have noticed about Richmond is that people—old ladies, in particular—are very concerned with who they're kin to. Doreen even has an old velvet-covered book with all her mother's people wrote down in it. She thinks it's the greatest thing to run her finger over the name of some kinfolk who once said howdy-do to George Washington or somebody from way back when.

That day, no sooner than we had got home, Doreen—"Aunt" Doreen—sat me down at her big desk where she'd laid out paper and ink.

"There's no time like the present to get started," she said. "Mind you use good grammar."

She has started in on me lately by trying to change the way I talk. Living with a school teacher is not easy. It would be quite a feather in her cap if I won the essay contest. It would reflect on her, and she would let on that I take after her.

Now, I can write good stories. There's not much I like better than a good story. I only had to think for a minute, then wrote—slow at first, then faster and faster. The ink blotched and smeared, but I didn't care. Ideas popped into my mind so fast I could hardly keep up with them.

I wrote how my Great-uncle John R. Forbes had almost won the War singlehanded for the Confederacy and saved General Lee from Yankee desperados but was kidnapped by pirates and sent all the way to France where Marie Antoinette and Joan of Arc befriended him and smuggled him back to Virginia disguised as an old lady, but the Yankees—who were shooting up women and children during a siege—shot him in the arm after he'd beaten near about a whole regiment senseless with his parasol and a walking cane, and how he'd barely made it back home to die, where he said he regretted having one one life to give for his country.

I thought it was my best story ever.

However, "Aunt" Doreen did not share my sentiments. As she read it, her pink face grew redder and redder until it looked like she might bust a gusset.

"Hannah!" she said. What are you trying to do? Bring shame and disgrace upon your family?"

"No, ma'am," I said. I cannot help that Doreen does not appreciate great stories.

"Think about what you write!" she said. "This is supposed to be a true story!"

I thought she was carrying on too much for no reason. She was a great one for carrying on. Some of the best stories I'd ever heard stretched the truth, or improved on the truth considerable.

"Some of it's true," I said. "Sort of."

"Very little!" she said. "Very little is even remotely close to the truth. Think of our family! You're entering this contest for the glory and honor of our family."

Patches on the Same Quilt

"No, I'm not," I blurted out without thinking. "I'm doing it for the five dollar gold piece."

I had secret plans to convert that gold piece to ready cash. Also, I wouldn't mind a little fame and attention for myself. That would show those prissy girls a thing or two. I didn't dare tell Doreen this. That might really set her off.

"The money? The money! Think of our family's reputation!" She was waving her arms wildly, not in a ladylike fashion at all. If Miss Emily Wicklin was to come walking in the door now and see Doreen, it would not be me who would bring disgrace to our family.

"Can't you think of some small true thing to write about?" she demanded. "Just one tiny speck of truth? Can't you do that? If you'd only apply your God-given talents...." Her voice drifted off and she went to the kitchen to fix herself a cup of tea to steady her nerves.

I don't know why "Aunt" Doreen always had to take on so. From the way she carried on, you'd have thought I'd been running buck-nekkid down Monument Avenue on Lee-Jackson Day.

Suddenly, in the quiet that followed Doreen's departure to the kitchen, I felt like I'd been horse-whipped. I searched my mind for ideas while I felt sorry for myself for being scolded so unjustly. Back home on the farm, no one would have treated me like this.

Daddy would have said to me, "If you don't get it right the first time, figure out what you did wrong and try again."

The first time he said that to me was when my first pony had pitched me into the fence. It took me three tries before I figured out not to clamp on so tight with my legs. I got skinned up considerable from the experience, but that pony never threw me again.

I crumpled up my story and heaved it across the room. She wanted a tiny speck of truth....

While I thought, I positioned a clean white sheet of paper in front of me. I stared at the blank paper a long time. I smoothed it with my hand a time or two. Finally, slowly, the seed of a thought planted itself inside my head, took root, and started growing. I picked up the pen and carefully dipped it in the inkwell. I bit my lower lip to keep the ink from blotching the page.

In my boldest hand, I began to write: *I know where a penny is hidden.*

Chapter 12
JOHNNY WEBSTER

TIMES ARE CHANGIN'

This mornin' my wife Emma says to me, "Johnny, do you realize this will be the last time all of you's gathered under the same roof?"

I hadn't thought of it, but doggone if she ain't right. Daddy o' course, is always here. Right now, he's settin' in the front room with William. Jus' settin', not sayin' a word. It's been right hard on him. Hannah's here, too, out in the barn somewhere. Cleanin' stalls, I reckon. Hard to believe she's in high school now and growin' like a weed. She's been back for over a year. Richmond jus' didn't work out for her or Doreen either one. Doreen come in from Richmond two days ago—she's layin' down upstairs. The strain is too much for her. She won't never one to bear up well under hardship.

Julia and her husband ought to be landin' at Woodrum Field in Roanoke anytime now. You couldn't git me on one of them planes, but she don't think a thing of it. I ain't seen Julia since I don't know when. She writes ever' so often, sayin' we ought to come up and see her and she'll show us a big time in New York. I don't reckon I'll ever take her up on it. I don't much care for crowds. 'Sides, who'd tend to things while I was gone. What with the war and all, good help is hard to come by. What I'd do without Hannah back here, I don't know. She's a big help, but still, she's just a girl yet.

Julia keeps in touch, though, you got to say that for her, even if she don't hardly come back much. When Emma and me was married, Julia sent us a big box full o' dishes and lace tablecloths and I don't know what all from one of those fancy New York stores. Emma was jus' tickled with it all. Doreen, now, to show you the difference between 'em, jus' sent us a few books and a old quilt. Emma didn't say nothin', but I could tell she was disappointed. She already had a whole hope chest full o' pieced quilts like that. I believe she was expectin' some fancy Richmond store-bought stuff. I reckon Doreen meant well enough.

When we knowed ever'one was comin', Emma made sure she got that quilt out and put it on the bed in the extry room so Doreen would know we was usin' it. Emma is like that. Even if her feelin's git hurt, she don't aim to hurt nobody else's. That's one of the things I admire most about her.

About me and Emma and how we happened to git married—I courted her pretty steady nigh through last winter and I finally told her flat out one Sunday when I took her home after preachin' if she wanted to see much o' me, she'd better marry me, for there was jus' too much to do on the farm for me to get a chance to slip off and see her ever' few days. Willie was gone by then, and o' course Daddy does what he can, but he's a old man and ought to rest more. What with the war and all, I'm sellin' all the beef I can raise, and wheat and tobacco, too. I hate to say it, but in some ways the war's been awful good for farmers.

Not in others, though, that's sure. Most able-bodied hands are gone—joined up or drafted, one. Right after Willie joined the Air Force, I thought about it some, but then I got that bad foot from where the horse stomped me when I was a kid. It don't bother me too much nowadays, 'cept in cold spells. It always lets me know when a storm is comin'. Main thing is, who'd keep the farm goin' with me gone. I doubt Daddy and Hannah could. 'Course Daddy can outwork me some days even though he's in his seventies. Not many days, but some.

Well, he was more'n a little put out with me when I bought that old Fordson tractor a few years back. I got a real good deal on it. Daddy ain't one for change even if it's for the best.

"We always worked mules," he said when he saw it.

"I know," I told him, "but times is changin'. We got to keep up."

When Willie left, it won't long 'til even Daddy had to admit that havin' a tractor made a difference. He never would learn to drive it, though. He jus' hated to admit we didn't need them mules as much as we once did. Oh, now we still keep a team to plow the hilly ground and such like, and Daddy's old buggy horse Noisy'll live forever it seems like. We can't git shut o' him. And Hannah's got her a ridin' horse or two, but most of the breedin' stock's been sold. The few mares we got left, we use to raise a few mules to sell. There's still a market for a mule.

But all them fine horses Daddy once bred are a thing of the past. Nobody wants horses anymore. It's a hard thing for him to let go of. I've tried to make him understand that there jus' ain't a market for horses. Even with all the gas rationin', people would still rather have theirselves a car. People want to get places fast, do things fast.

I've cleared a lot of land with that tractor, made good grazin' land, good hayfields. I cleaned up a lot o' that scrub pine that had come up and took over. Got the brush off the bottoms. They jus' as green now. It's a big satisfaction to me to see purty land that's took care of.

Gettin' back to Emma, you couldn't ask for a better woman. Good cook, hard worker. Our first one's due in five months. Daddy's first grandbaby. I believe he always did hope that Doreen or Julia would give him one, but Doreen never married and Julia could never have any.

'Course, there was Willie, but he never would settle down and marry. Always got to be on the go. Never stuck to anything long enough to put down roots. Always off somewhere. When him and Daddy was goin' to the big horse shows, Daddy had hopes Willie'd be the one to stay and keep on with the horses. But the horses won't enough for Willie. Whatever he done, he always craved something more.

He took off to West Virginia and worked the mines for awhile. Went to Roanoke and worked for the railroad for a spell, then the silk mill. Before long, he'd come back home and then go off again. He never found what he was lookin' for. Then he joined the Air Force. Learned to fly airplanes. Sent us a picture one time of him sittin' up there in the cockpit jus' grinnin' like he was somethin'. Finally found something fast enough to suit him. Now he's back home again. This time he'll stay.

Anyway, I worked all mornin' up on the hill. Got ever'thing ready. We jus' got to wait for ever'one to git here.

They say Willie was a big hero before he was shot down. He nearly made it back, they told us. His plane was all shot up and he was wounded. He almost made it back to base before he must've lost consciousness and crashed.

I reckon we was lucky to get his body back at all. The gover'ment sent a little box with his medals in it. I don't know whether to bury them with him or put them away somewhere as a reminder that Willie finally settled down and done somethin'.

I reckon I'll jus' put 'em away 'til Daddy gits used to him bein' gone. Daddy'll be proud of them medals some day.

I dug Willie's grave right behind where Mama is buried. Took me all mornin', but it was somethin' I was bound to do.

He couldn't ask for a nicer place to spend Eternity—high up on that hill so near to the sky.

Chapter 13
ANNE LEE WEBSTER

LAST MEMORY

Whenever I think of November, 1963, I can't help thinking of funerals—first Grandaddy's, then President Kennedy's. The two men didn't have much in common—other than both of them being named John F.—except for the horse in the funeral procession.

I'd always thought Grandaddy would live forever. He was an old man for as long as he lived—at least for as long as I lived. He'd lived in the same house—our house—ever since he was a young man. He was ninety-five when he died. That month—that year—I was nineteen and a sophomore majoring in art at Richmond Professional Institute.

I remember I was sitting in the cafeteria in the basement of Founder's Hall—the residence hall where I also lived. It was the small, drab cafeteria—the one where the art students usually hang out—off the main one. The walls were that ghastly gold-yellow tile half-way up and then blue-painted plaster above. The tables were heavy wood with formica easy-to-wipe-clean tops. All in all, it was neither an appetizing nor an aesthetically pleasing place.

I'd just finished a three-hour painting class and I'd come straight to lunch without having gone upstairs to my room on the second floor to change. I was wearing paint-spattered Levi's, and—since young ladies weren't to be seen on campus in jeans in the unenlightened times of 1963—a paint-spattered trench coat to cover them. I was sitting with some other equally paint-spattered kids from class and having an intense discussion about a Ferlinghetti poem. I was picking at the remains of my hamburger—we called them *booger-burgers*—and sipping black coffee. As I drained the dregs from my cup, I glanced up and there was Aunt Doreen, looking around nervously, looking seriously out of place.

Aunt Doreen's real short—five two, maybe—and she always wears her reddish-white hair piled up high on her head so she'll look taller. She has more hair than face. She was wearing a dark green tweed suit with a black velvet collar and her customary high heels. She was wringing her black gloves as her eyes darted around, searching.

As my mind was making a sketch of her—she looked so out of place among us grubby students, a kid at the table pointed at her and remarked that one of the old ladies must have escaped from the Chesterfield across the street—the Chesterfield's an apartment building inhabited by little old ladies. Aunt Doreen eats in their tearoom sometimes. Now that she's retired, she has a lot of loose ends in her life.

Anyhow, at that moment she spotted me and called out, "Anne-Lee! Anne-Lee!" and started toward me, the staccato sound of her high heels breaking the silence that had suddenly descended. My friends, who'd been crowded conspiratorially around the table, parted like the Red Sea for Moses and let her through.

"Oh, Anne-Lee!" she wailed. Her eyes were red, so you could tell she'd been crying. "You've got to come with me! Papa died last evening."

I didn't know what to say. My friends fading into the background were equally mute.

"I just spoke to your housemother," she continued. "She thought perhaps I'd find you down here. I've already called Dean Gladding. It's all arranged for you to go."

There was no question, then, that I'd go. When I stood up, she frowned at the paint stains on my trench coat.

"Let me get my things," I said. I added, "Come on up," not knowing what else to do with her. She followed me up the stairs.

I stopped at the lobby desk and collected a handful of phone messages—all from Aunt Doreen, who must have spent the entire morning trying to reach me. We climbed the long staircase to the second floor, turned right, and went into the second room.

We went through the door as my room-mate Janine, a drama major, was staring intently into the dresser mirror and rehearsing her lines for an up-coming production of *The Crucible*. She was doing the court-room scene—I must have heard it fifty times, so I pretty much knew it by heart—where the girls get hysterical. She'd been working on her timing all week.

Janine, concentrating fiercely, screamed and backed up, nearly colliding with Aunt Doreen. Aunt Doreen, though nonplused, quickly regained her composure—she'd spent the better part of her life regaining her composure, Aunt Hannah once told me—and stared at the wall, only to have her eyes assaulted by the near-life size nude figure studies taped there. I'd been working on them the night before. Having nowhere else to look, she stared at the floor and chewed her lower lip while I threw stuff I thought I'd need into my suitcase and explained to Janine—whose concentration was now broken—where I was going and why. Aunt Doreen and I then hurried out.

Her white Bonneville was parked at the curb on Franklin Street. She handed me the keys. She was too upset, she declared, to drive. I took them, tossed my suitcase into the back seat where Aunt Doreen had carefully laid out a black wool dress—still in the dry cleaner's bag, and slid into the driver's seat.

Driving the Bonneville through Friday afternoon traffic on Franklin Street was like piloting a battleship up the James River. Thank goodness she had power steering. I flipped on the radio and tuned it to WLEE. Some new English rock group was singing a mindless song with a lot of "yeah-yeah-yeah's" in it. I tapped out the rhythm on the steering wheel as I drove. Aunt Doreen reached out and snapped the radio off.

"I hardly think that's appropriate," she said.

It was going to be a long drive.

I circled Monroe Park, cut down some back streets, and headed for the Lee Bridge. I didn't ask her what route she wanted to take. She'd tell me soon enough if the one I picked didn't suit her, I was sure. I decided to head toward Appomattox on Route 60, and then swing south through Rustburg and Altavista and Gretna to pick up Route 40 for Penhook. It was a little longer than taking Route 360, but it would get me out of Richmond traffic much sooner, so time-wise it was about the same.

Aunt Doreen was quiet for a while. So was I. I really wanted the radio on. Then she started to talk. "It is Death that separates us," she said in her best English teacher voice," and Death that connects us. We always come together after a death."

I didn't know what to say. I don't guess she expected a response because she continued—just like she was lecturing a class or something.

"I remember when my Grandma Julia died," she said. "She'd had a stroke and never got over it. Folks came from everywhere. Distant relatives that I'd never even seen came from Baltimore. My sister Julia and her new husband came. All the neighbors. Everyone."

She paused. I kept driving.

"And Great-uncle Ezra in Danville. His heart had been giving him trouble and he'd been housebound for some time. It grieved him that he couldn't go out and see the horses. His housekeeper found him. He was sitting in his big burgundy wing-chair in his study and staring at a painting of a stallion he used to have, she said. I was in my last year of teacher's college then. Grandmother Cabell took me out of school and we went by train. Papa was there. And Mama-Annie. Even though it was tobacco-time, they took off and went. I suppose that was the farthest Mama-Annie had ever been from home. She never liked to go anywhere. Papa said he just had to come. He owed it to Uncle Ezra. Papa said had it not been for Uncle Ezra, his life would have been very different."

I didn't ask how. Aunt Doreen didn't say. She moved on to the next death.

"And three years later, Grandmother Cabell herself was dead. A kidney stone—or a gallstone—I forget just which. I was teaching at St. Catherine's when it happened. I remember I was lecturing about 'Thanatopsis.' The headmistress came in and asked me to go into the hall. She didn't want me to cry in front of my students, I suppose. She told me to go on home where I was needed, that someone else would take my class. Grandmother Cabell was the last of the Pemberton line. Uncle Ezra never married. Grandmother Cabell once said something about his being betrothed before the War, but his sweetheart died very young. While he was away, I think."

I gripped the steering wheel a little tighter and kept my mind on driving. I could do without Aunt Doreen's morbid litany.

Fortunately, Aunt Doreen was quiet for most of the three hours. Near Appomattox, she spoke of one of our long-dead relatives—"Papa was named for him"—who was wounded in March of 1865—"March the second," she believed—"in Waynesboro when Jubal Early's troops were attacked by George Custer's forces. Though gravely wounded, our brave kinsman managed to avoid being taken prisoner, though many valiant Confederate soldiers were, and accompanied Early toward Richmond to assist General Lee," Aunt Doreen explained in her best school teacher manner.

Aunt Doreen was, no doubt, a real credit to the Daughters of the Confederacy. She'd once even served a term as recording secretary, one of the "proudest moments" of her life.

"You know,"she confided, "I was never sorry about what the Indians did to Custer. I think he deserved it."

Aunt Doreen was usually too much of a lady to show vindictiveness. This was a side of her that I hadn't noticed before.

I'd lived with Aunt Doreen for the first semester of my freshman year. It had been a strain on both of us. Aunt Doreen had nurtured a vain hope that, since I'd be in Richmond, I would attend Westhampton—not RPI, and that I'd major in something genteel—English literature, maybe—not something as messy as fine art; but I had already made up my mind. Aunt Hannah, who'd also lived a stint with Aunt Doreen in her earlier years, had warned me—"Forewarned is forearmed," she said—about Aunt Doreen's pretensions to society. I made it through my first semester. That was all I could stand. For second semester, I signed up for several night classes and managed to convince

Daddy that I'd be safer in a dorm than on the streets of Richmond after dark. Even Aunt Doreen had to agree. I think by then she'd given up on ever rehabilitating me into a proper young lady. Aunt Hannah told me that Aunt Doreen had probably worn herself out trying to civilize her and didn't have much fight left in her. At any rate, Aunt Doreen still called me every week or so "to see how you're getting on" and to occasionally invite me to lunch at the Chesterfield tearoom, which I usually declined if I could find an excuse.

It was dusk when I turned the Bonneville off Route 40 and onto the gravel road that leads home. I slowed down so I wouldn't sling gravel and scratch Aunt Doreen's car. Of course, she wouldn't say a word if I did, but she'd frown in that way she has and chew her lower lip. Soon I could see the silhouettes of Daddy's Herefords grazing behind the lines of barbed wire and could pick out the dark shapes of the old tobacco barns in the distance. Before we came to our house, we passed the cabin where Aunt Hannah and Uncle Jack live. A single kerosene lamp burned in the window, but there was no sign of anybody at home.

Aunt Hannah's cabin is actually an old tenant house. Outside, it looks like a shack. Inside—well, it's hard to describe—it's a library, an artist's studio, and a museum all rolled into one. It used to draw me like a magnet when I was a kid. Every chance I got, I'd run up the hill to visit Aunt Hannah. Everyone's heard of her—she writes children's books. She's been a writer ever since she was ten and won first prize in a writing contest. She still has her prize—a five-dollar gold piece.

Uncle Jack illustrates her books—"She only married me because she can't draw worth a hoot herself, and she hates to spend the money to hire an artist," he likes to joke.

He's the one who told me about the art program at RPI in the first place. In fact, he's the one who encouraged me to become an artist. When I was little, Aunt Hannah would read me what she'd written, and then I'd try to draw it before Uncle Jack did. He usually beat me, though. Mama and Daddy probably would've been against my studying art if they hadn't seen how

Uncle Jack makes a pretty good living from it. That convinced them to let me give it a try.

Aunt Hannah and Uncle Jack could probably live anywhere they wanted, but they chose the tenant house. Only one room has electricity—the room they finally added so they'd have a kitchen and indoor bathroom.

"People made do without electricity for hundreds of years and did just fine," I remember Aunt Hannah once said.

"Hummph," Aunt Doreen said in reply. "I tried my best. I couldn't civilize her."

Grandaddy once told me that Aunt Hannah's house dated back to slave times. A former slave, Henry Washington Forbes, lived in it for the better part of his life. He's buried near it. His headstone is the only one in the old slave cemetery with a name on it. Some of the other headstones are worn so smooth, they look like ancient sculpture. Aunt Hannah plants flowers all over that graveyard every spring. Aunt Doreen cannot understand why.

As I drove past their house, it occurred to me that of course they wouldn't be home, they'd be down at our house with Aunt Julia and Uncle Tarlie—who'd probably be in from New York by now—and my younger brother J.D. and my little sister Sarah. Soon the familiar outline of our old house that had been added to and expanded over the years loomed into view. Someone—Mama, probably—had left the porch light on for us.

After we'd been welcomed and hugged and fed and our things brought in from the car, Aunt Doreen had to know, "How did Papa—?" you could tell she hated to say the word "die." It would make it too final, too real.

"Well," Mama started, and you could tell she'd had practice telling it over and over all day, "It was right warm yesterday, so he reckoned he'd sit out for a while in the side yard. You know how he always liked to sit there. Where he could see over the fields and all. Well, Hannah was ridin' that new mare she's been foolin' with. He wanted to watch that, you know. He always did like a horse. So he took him a chair out and propped it back against that big old maple out there and set hisself down to watch Hannah."

"He waved to me," Aunt Hannah said. "I saw him wave. After I'd warmed up Lady, I rode her on up the road. I turned around just before I crested the hill and waved back at him. He waved again. That was the last time I saw him alive."

"When he didn't come in for supper," Mama picked up again, "I sent your Daddy out to get him."

Finally it was Daddy's turn to add his part: "He was settin' there in his chair jus' like he'd dropped off to sleep. He was even smilin'. I put my hand on him to wake him up. He was cold."

"Your Daddy come runnin' back in, his face jus' as white it liked to scared me. We didn't know what to do," Mama continued, "so we called up the funeral home and they came right out and got him. Then we started callin' folks we knew."

I listened quietly while they talked over the little details—what he might have said last and to whom, what he wore, what he did earlier in the day—as if they were trying to hold onto something that had already gone. This was the first time I'd faced death up close and at home. Everyone I'd ever known to die before hadn't been real close kin or else had been sick as well as old. I don't ever remember Grandaddy being sick. I couldn't think of him dead—it was easier to think that he was just asleep in his bedroom off the kitchen, and that's why he wasn't out here with us. He was in his room, I told myself, not lying in a coffin fifteen miles away.

We went out to Rocky Mount to see him that night, and again the next day—Saturday—for his funeral. They had laid Grandaddy out in the largest room in the funeral home. I think Daddy was proud that he was successful enough to be able to afford to do this for Grandaddy. The funeral drew a huge crowd. All the seats in the chapel were filled, and people stood in the hallway to listen. Afterwards, more cars than I could count were in the procession. Daddy drove Doreen's Bonneville behind the hearse. Mama, Aunt Doreen, Aunt Julia, and her husband rode with him. Sarah, J.D., Aunt Hannah, and I rode in the second car—Daddy's Fairlane—that Uncle Jack drove. All the others came after, each with their headlights on. I kept turning around to watch them. There were more cars than I could count.

Patches on the Same Quilt

When we got to the farm, the funeral director worried that he didn't know how he could get the casket up the hill to the graveyard where yesterday some workers had dug the grave. He knew the hearse wouldn't make it, and "Mr. Webster's a mighty big man for the pall bearers to tote so far up a steep grade like that."

Aunt Hannah had already anticipated that. She and Uncle Jack pulled an old wagon out of the shed next to the barn. Then they brought out Aunt Hannah's black mare, Lady Luck, who'd been standing in her stall, and harnessed her. Lady's eyes rolled back as Aunt Hannah backed her between the shafts; she wasn't used to being a harness horse. She pranced some, but Aunt Hannah stayed by her head and talked softly to her as Uncle Jack hooked up the check rein. Aunt Hannah patted and soothed and comforted her, so by the time the pall bearers had loaded the casket onto the wagon, the mare was settled and ready to go. Just before she climbed into the driver's seat, Aunt Hannah left Uncle Jack to hold Lady while she ran back into the shed and returned with a set of old brass sleigh bells that she fastened onto Lady's harness. Uncle Jack helped Aunt Hannah onto the wagon seat and climbed up beside her, and together they drove the wagon, rattling and jingling, up the hill to the graveyard—almost like they were going to a picnic instead of a burying. The rest of us made our way on foot—a long line of people of all ages. When we were all assembled on the hill top, it seemed there were even more people than had been at the funeral home. A group of colored people, quietly watching, stood off to one side. Some of them had been Grandaddy's tenants at one time or another; some were neighbors. All were friends. My eyes searched the crowd, looking at people's faces, making mental sketches. Some day, I knew, I'd paint this scene.

"One generation passeth away," the preacher read, "and another generation cometh; but the earth endureth forever."

Then Grandaddy's casket was lowered into the space between his two wives. Before he was covered with shovelfuls of sweet-smelling damp earth, Aunt Hannah reached into her pocket, took out a penny, and tossed it into the grave. I heard it clatter on the casket. Lady whinnied, and I heard the echo of her whinny from far below, like another horse off in the distance was answering her. After the grave was covered, people stood in little clusters to talk, to remember.

An old black lady suddenly appeared before me, looked me in the face, and said, "I know who you are. I know your people." She nodded, as if to approve of me somehow, and moved on. She came and went so quickly, it scared me a little.

I rode back down the hill in the wagon with Aunt Hannah and Uncle Jack and Aunt Julia and my brother and sister. Aunt Doreen had been invited but declined, preferring to pick her way down in her high heels instead. I guess she thought it was undignified to ride down in an old farm wagon.

Aunt Julia began to sing, "Shall We Gather At the River," and we all joined in, and the people walking behind us, too, and the whole hillside rang with our singing. Somehow to me, it seemed just right on this warm Saturday afternoon in early November, with the last of autumn's leaves still clinging to the trees, to go rattling and jingling and singing down the hill, where—in a few hours—we'd soon separate and get on with our individual lives again until the time came for the next one to take his or her place on the hill.

It must have been then that the thought occurred to me—"I know who I am. I know my people." I was *who* I was because of who I was. Because of my people—the ones here around me and the ones on the hill, the generations that had passed before.

After Aunt Hannah and Uncle Jack unhitched the wagon, put it away, and curried Lady Luck, we all gathered in the front room—the old front room of the original log part of the house—where there's a little window cut by the chimney. From that window, you could see the graveyard if the trees hadn't grown up in the way. Aunt Julia sat down at the piano and played some of the old hymns and we all sang "Amazing Grace," Grandaddy's favorite which we'd sung earlier today at the funeral. After that, we sang "Blest Be the Tie That Binds" and "Will the Circle Be Unbroken." We were ready to sing another one, but then Aunt Julia played some kind of classical music, her fingers dancing on the keys with all the flourishes. Suddenly she stopped playing.

Patches on the Same Quilt

"I don't know why I played that Mozart sonata," she apologized. "It just popped into my head. It hardly seems appropriate...."

I'm not into classical music, but it sounded fine to me.

I don't remember much about the rest of the evening. We had lots of company and plenty to eat because everyone around had brought food when they first heard. I do remember ideas for paintings kept forming in my brain, ideas that I'd tuck away in some far corner of my mind. Some I confess I've forgotten already. I remember I wanted to take something tangible back with me, something to remind me of here, of this place and this time—some last memory I could hold on to. Mama went to her cedar chest and got me out a quilt.

"I don't know if this is what you want or not," she said. "It's old, but it ain't in real good shape. You're welcome to it if you want it."

Most of the patches were so faded you could hardly tell what color they had been originally, and some of the stitches were broken. It looked like the stitches had originally been sewn to make some kind of a design or pictures. This quilt had been washed over and over to a soft smoothness you can't get in store-bought blankets, and it smelled wonderful—of soap and woodsmoke and mama's cedar chest. Someday, I'll put this quilt in a painting, I told myself. I folded it carefully, reverently. It was too big to fit in my suitcase.

It was dark when I finally went to bed, a dark that you only find in the country—I've never seen it in Richmond—but there were stars, thousands of stars, stars that don't shine in Richmond either. I lay awake for a long time, thinking about this day and my part in it. I decided maybe from now on, I'd be more serious about my art-work and my studies. Somehow, knowing your beginning and your ending makes you work a little harder on the middle. This day I'd seen both my beginning and ending. I was suddenly aware—really aware for the first time—of my own mortality. There was a place for me in the graveyard, just as there'd been for all those already buried up there, just as there'd be for all of us under this house's tin roof. I understood now why the middle was so important. When at last I slept, it was a long and dreamless sleep.

The next afternoon, on the way back to Richmond, Aunt Doreen was a lot more talkative—like a great weight had been lifted and she was free. She talked about life in the old days when she was a little girl on the farm, and the pony she used to ride—"the prettiest little sorrel pony you ever saw!"—and how Aunt Julia would bang out tunes on the forbidden piano when she thought no one was listening, and when her brothers Johnny and William were born.

"You know," she said, "I just remembered something from when I was just a little tiny girl. Julia was still a baby. We—Mama was holding Julia, and Papa was holding a shovel—we stood out in the pasture and had a funeral for Papa's horse. Can you imagine? A funeral for a horse. I remember all of us crying—even Papa. It was almost dark when he finished burying the horse. I think Mama sang. Then Papa picked me up and carried me back across the field to the house in the dark. I wonder why I never remembered that until now."

I couldn't answer. Then Aunt Doreen told me about when she came to Richmond and about the quilt. My great-great grandmother had made it—the last one before she died. My great grandmother had given it to Aunt Doreen when she went to Richmond, and she had kept it for years to hand down to a daughter of her own when she had one.

"Well, I never married, so I never had a daughter to pass it to. When your father married your mother, I gave it to them as a wedding present. It's right that it goes to you now," she explained. After that she was quiet. So was I. We rode wrapped in our separate silences the rest of the way back.

At the dorm, I pulled the Bonneville to the curb and got my things out of the back seat. Aunt Doreen slid over to take the wheel. We promised to keep in touch, and I remember she said her good-by in a way so unlike her, in the old-fashioned country way: "Well, you better come go with me."

Two weeks later, President Kennedy was shot. In the green-walled East parlor of Founder's Hall, I sat packed elbow to elbow with most of the girls in the dorm and watched his funeral on television. Most of the girls sniffed or sobbed quietly, a few wept openly, but I sat stone-faced, stoically thinking, *I do not really know this man. He may have been my President, but he is not my people.*

The procession that passed in front of our eyes as we watched the small, black and white screen seemed so far away. Then the riderless horse came into view.

I left the parlor, ran up the steps, flung myself on my bed, wrapped my quilt around me, and let my tears flow.

Chapter 14
ROSE ELLA

PLAY "MOAT'S ARK" FOR ME

A hunnerd years old today!

People make a fuss when you git that old. Folks here at Franklin Manor Home for Adults had me a party. Put a little paper hat on my head. Got me a cake an' sang Happy Birthday Rose-Ella. Made my picture an' gonna put it in the paper. Young white girl come from that Roanoke Times paper an' want to write about me. Say to me, Rose-Ella, tell me about your life. Now what I gonna say to her? It a life. I done live most of it. Some memories still clear as the day I live 'em an' some done fade. Some I reckon done improve with age. I got regrets, same as mos' people. I got joys, too.

What you do with yourself all day? she ask me. I say mostly I sit an' wait. I look out at that Route 220 road. Watch all them cars goin' by real fast. Too fast for me. Maybe I live so long 'cause I went slower. Ever'body did back then.

That not what she want to hear, I kin tell. She purse her red lips tight an' try agin. What you do when you a young person? she say.

What I do, I tell her. I grow up same as ever'body didn't die young. I grow up an' then I grow old. That God's plan. Born, grow up, grow old, die. It that simple. What not so simple is how. That the thing. How. Some folks better at it than others. I done about average so far, I tell her.

She kindly squirm in her chair, but she busy writin' down ever' word on a little pad of paper. It give me time to think while I wait for her to catch up. I tell her, I born Rose Ella Lily

May Daisy Pearl Violet Pangburn. She write that down. I tell her that my Mamma—Granny Odell the Baby-Catcher—give me all the purties' names of all the purties' things she know 'cause I her first-born an' she gittin' old when she have me an' she think I gonna be her only chile, only I ain't. Few years after me come my baby sister, an' Mamma done use up all the good names.

Paper lady smile an' look like she interested. So I go on. I tell her that Mamma finally name my sister Allis. Not much of a name. She a skinny little puny thing. When she little, I tease her. I say Allis is all lice. That make her cry an' run tell Mamma. Mamma smack me good. While later, I start up agin. I say real low, Allis is all lice, she not nice, she eat mice. She run tell Mamma agin. Tell I say she eat mice. Mamma smack her this time. Tell Allis if she don' know she don' eat mice then she foolish.

The paper lady stop writin' an' jus' listen. I stop talkin'. Go on, she say, tell me more about Allis.

I think to myself how Allis foolish. Shif'less too. She raised right—same as me—but it don' take. Won' work for what she want. She a fool for trinkets an' shiny things an' sweet-talkin' men. Not me. I always work hard an' do right.

Paper lady wait. I don' want to talk bad about my sister. I say I lose track of her long time ago. She live fast. She probably long dead. I don' know.

Then tell me about your Mamma, paper lady say. She ask me, what is a baby-catcher? I tell her that is woman who help other women have their babies. When I jus' a little bitty chap, I ask Mamma why she always goin' off. She tell me she go an' catch babies. I tell ever'body that my Mamma a baby-catcher. Before long, ever'body call her that. Granny Odell the Baby-Catcher. I think for a long time that she jus' go stan' in a field with her arms up an' Jesus fling down babies from up on a cloud way up near Heaven an' Mamma catch 'em an' han' 'em out to ladies who want 'em. When I older an' start goin' round with Mamma, I find out it not how I think. Not near as nice. She catch white an' colored babies both. It all the same, she tell me. Each one come out red an' wrinkled when she first catch it. Ever'body start off exactly the same. Well, harder for some than others, maybe. Some she got to pull out on account they want to come backwards. Maybe they see how hard life gonna be, they don' want to face it. I don' much blame 'em.

Paper lady smile a big smile. Then she want to know what were some big things in my life. I tell her, won' no big things. Jus' a lot of little things pieced together.

Oh, she say, but you seen the first cars, an' all them wars, an' even a man walk on the moon. What I think of that? She sound all excited.

I got to tell her I ain' never see much of that. While I growin' up, cars edge out the horses, but a horse go about as fast as I care to go. All them wars happen far off. Never touch me. Man on the moon jus' some little pictures on TV. I watch TV some, but I kin do without it. I kin tell she gittin' real disappointed. Maybe her boss be mad if she don' git somethin' fancier than what I say. She try agin. Ask me if I remember goin' round with my Mamma.

I tell her, yes ma'am I do. When I old enough, Mamma fix it so I git job lookin' after chaps an' keepin' house 'til lady that have baby git rested up. It a good job. Better'n catchin' babies. Best thing, I never stay so long I wear out my welcome. Most women, they ask for me special. They always say to Mamma, Where Rose-Ella? You bring Rose-Ella? They always glad to see me. Sometimes slip me a little extra money above what the husban' pay. Usually it a happy time.

Paper lady writin' jus' as fast. I stop talkin', let her catch up. Suddenly, I think of a time it not so happy. I try to hold my mind back from thinkin' it, but too late. I think it anyway.

I recollect one spring I go with Mamma to Miz Dorie's when she about ready. She already birthed two little gals an' done jus' fine. They the apple of their Daddy's eye. So is Miz Dorie. Mr. John jus' dote on her. She real purty. Hair almos' red but not quite. An' sing! She put the angels to shame she sing so good. Always sing to her babies. Mr. John play the piano an' she sing. He only man I know back then play a piano.

Paper lady finish writin' an' look like she expec' more story. I play like I doze off 'cause my mind won' turn loose this memory. Paper lady wait. I peep ever' so often an' see what she doin'.

Mos' men, when they wife due, they run off. Maybe git drunk. Not Mr. John. He stay close by in front room an' play on that piano for all he worth. Ever' time pain hit, Miz Dorie squeeze my han' like she gonna wring it off an' call to Mr. John, play "Moat's Ark" for me! Play "Moat's Ark!" over an' over. I ain' never hear of this tune anywhere else. I don' believe it got words on account I never hear Miz Dorie sing it. It sound somethin' like church music. Only differnt. Mr. John's fingers jus' fly over them piano keys.

Miz Dorie call out over an' over, play "Moat's Ark!" Myself, I never hear of any ark-man but Noah. Never hear of Moat. He not in the Bible.

Paper lady catch me peepin' an' know I awake. What you thinkin' 'bout? she say.

I tell her I studyin' 'bout a clock a lady name of Miz Dorie have in her front room that she wind ever' mornin'. It got a little bird who come out an' chirp ever' so often. He chirp a lot at noon, then he got to rest up. Only chirp one time after that. He rest up, he chirp more. Miz Dorie got to wind that clock ever' day with a little key to keep that bird chirpin'. Mr. John's Mamma give them that clock on their weddin' day. That what Miz Dorie once tell me.

I stop talkin' 'cause I know what memory gonna come next an' I don' want to say it out loud. Sayin' it out loud make it too much so. Want to hold it to myself. I play like I doze off agin.

The day Miz Dorie die, she don' wind that clock. I never agin hear that bird chirp. That a sad, sad day.

Mamma know right off Miz Dorie don' look right. It even a full moon what ought to bring a baby out, but it don' work this time. Mamma put both a ax an' a butcher knife under the bed to cut Miz Dorie's pains, but that don' work neither. Miz Dorie hurt awful bad. You kin see. Her face so white. Whiter than usual white folks. Her eyes look like nobody home inside. She spend most all day tryin' to birth that baby. All day she wring my han' an' call out to Mr. John for him to play "Moat's Ark" an' all day he keep playin' it. Over an' over. Finally Mamma git

Patches on the Same Quilt

baby turned so he come out. She almos' catch him too late 'cause he all blue in his face. Mamma blow her breath into him. She make him live. All this time, Mr. John he keep playin' that piano. Mamma hold up baby so Miz Dorie kin see. She look at her baby boy an' she smile a smile jus' like a angel an' then she die. Jus' slip away. Mamma han' baby to me an' then she go tell Mr. John that Miz Dorie gone. He stop playin'. He never agin play that piano as far as I know.

I peep at paper lady. She lookin' over what she already write down an' she don' pay no attention to me. The wors' part of the memory over. I go on an' think it to the end.

I recollect I stay on an' keep house for Mr. John after Miz Dorie buried. When she not quite three months dead, Mr. John up an' bring home a gal he hardly know an' he marry her. He say to me, thank you Rose-Ella for all you do, an' he pay me. That gal a big strong gal. She have her two or three babies jus' as easy. I come help ever' time. But Mr. John never agin play that piano an' that bird never chirp agin.

Finally that memory let go of me, but it done wore me out. I open my eyes. Paper lady lookin' right at me. What you thinkin' now? she ask.

I tell her I think of a big thing after all. That clock of Miz Dorie's with the bird who chirp, I tell her, that a big thing to me a long time ago. Still is. I tell her I think maybe we all somethin' like God's clocks an' someday He too busy to wind some of us up—or maybe He forget—an' that the day we die. Our bird don' chirp no more.

Paper lady git funny look on her face when I tell her this. She start gatherin' up her things. Is there anything you wish for? she want to know.

That easy, I tell her. When my time come to be buried along side Mamma up on the hill back home, I wish somebody come an' plant daisies an' roses an' violets on me. All the purty flowers. Paper lady nod, but she don' answer me back right off. Finally she say, that all?

Well, I say. One more thing. When my time come, maybe somebody could play "Moat's Ark" for me.

She smile like she don' know what to say. Then she rush out. I reckon she never hear of Moat.

After she go, I so wore out I lay down an' doze off an' sleep. I dream a dream so real, when I wake up it seem like a memory of somethin' that really happen.

I dream I hear a bird chirp at the window. When I git up to go see, there is Moat in his ark. He motion to me to git in, an' I do, an' we sail off. Up ahead is a angel look jus' like Miz Dorie with her hair all unpinned an' fallin' down ever' which way. She have on a long white robe an' gold wings. She point the way an' Moat follow along, steerin' that ark jus' as calm. Behind us is a angel look jus' like my sister. She have on a shiny silver robe an' silver wings that shine so bright, she light up the whole ark for us. We sail an' sail. Way up in the clouds. We stop at ever' cloud an' some babies git on each time 'til finally we have us a whole ark-load of babies.

Then we sail up to a big cloud near Heaven where Jesus is. One by one I han' them babies up to Jesus. He smile an' thank me. Then one by one he fling them babies down to my Mamma who is standin' in a big field with her arms held out. All this time piano music is playin'.

It sound somethin' like church music. Only differnt.

Chapter 15
JOANNA ROLLINS

FULL CIRCLE

My Great-aunt Hannah says she will buy me a horse or a pony when I am able to canter one of the school horses all the way around the ring without stopping. I have always wanted a horse of my own. I take riding lessons once a week at Hunting Hills Stables right by the very same highway that you drive on to get to where Aunt Hannah lives. We—my mommy and daddy—drive on this same highway to get to our condo on the lake where we go on week-ends.

Our condo is not far from the farm where Aunt Hannah lives, and I'd much rather go to the farm than to the lake if you want to know the truth of it. Mommy is an artist and she says she gets good ideas when she sits on the porch and looks at the lake. I do not see how you get ideas from just sitting, but she says that she does.

I think it is so boring. We don't even have a beach like at Myrtle Beach where we went once, so I cannot even go swimming. Mommy says since there's no lifeguard and there are still big trees down in the lake bottom where farms once were and the lake is a mile deep in some places and she worries about me drowning, that is why I can't go swimming in the lake.

So we go to the condo and sit, until I complain enough so that Mommy drives me over to visit Aunt Hannah so she can get some peace and quiet.

Aunt Hannah lives on a farm that has been in our family since nearly forever. My grandparents live on the same farm, but instead of living in the big house with Aunt Hannah, they live in a trailer up near the road. They are very old, and living in the trailer is easier for them because they don't have many steps to go up and down, and they can get out easy and see who goes along the road and everything. When we go to Aunt Hannah's, we always stop in and see my grandparents first. They always say, "My, Joanna, how you've grown!" I hate that, but I don't say anything. Aunt Hannah is old, too, but not as old as they are and she doesn't act old, and she never ever says how I've grown. Grandma and Grandpa always talk about people I've never met and who are mostly dead anyway.

Aunt Hannah likes to have me visit. She says so. She is a writer and makes up funny rhymes with our names—*Joanna* and *Hannah*—and *banana* and *piano* and all kinds of silly words. She makes me laugh. Some of the books she wrote are in my school library.

I go to Huff Lane School where I am in the fourth grade. On library day, I always go find Aunt Hannah's books and look at them, even though most of them are written for second graders and not good readers like me. When other kids laugh at me for getting easy books, I tell them that my great-aunt wrote those books, but they do not believe me. I don't care because I know what is true even if they don't.

I want to be a writer just like Aunt Hannah. I want to live on a farm like she does and have a horse like she used to before she got too old and her horse got even older and died with its head in her arms. That is what she once told me. I would settle for a pony though, and I don't ever plan to get so old that I can't ride. When I tell her this, she laughs.

Mommy says taking a riding lesson once a week is plenty and I should be thankful for that because poor children don't even get that much, and when I'm older and have a job I can get all the horses and ponies I want. Besides that, I have a dog which is more than a lot of other children have.

Mommy does not understand. She used to live on the farm when she was my age, the same farm where Aunt Hannah lives now. Mommy says living on a farm is not so much fun when you live there every day and have chores and can't see your friends whenever you want because they live too far away. She likes living in Roanoke where she does freelance work for ad agencies, but it isn't really free because they pay her. That is where the money comes from for my riding lessons and to support my dog Boo, she says, so I'd better be glad we live in town. I say Daddy could pay for my lessons because he's a lawyer and people say they make lots of money and why can't he buy me a horse if he makes so much money. Mommy rolls her eyes and says that not all lawyers make lots of money.

The reason I got riding lessons is because I begged her so much for a horse. Mommy thought that if I could see how much trouble horses and ponies were, I wouldn't want one so much.

She was wrong. Now I want one more than ever. I have been taking lessons since March. There are two other girls in my riding group—Mary and Angie. Like me, they had begged for a horse, too. At first we had to ride inside the barn because it was always too cold and windy to ride in the big ring outside. Then it rained a lot. Carla—the riding instructor for beginners—said she always started lessons in the barn anyway, so we weren't missing anything.

We learned how to mount up and hold the reins and sit in the saddle properly, and we also learned how to put the saddle and bridle on. You call it tacking up. All three of us had a lot of trouble learning this. Tidbit, the pony I usually rode because I was the smallest and so was he, would close his mouth and refuse to open it for the bit. It took me a long time to figure out how to get him to open his mouth. You have to put your thumb in the corner of his mouth and pry it open. It sounds nasty, but it works. When his mouth is open, you lift the bit in. You don't want to bang his teeth. He probably has had his teeth banged by other kids and that is why he doesn't want to open his mouth. It is hard to tighten the girth on his saddle, too, and for a long time, I would get it too loose and the saddle would slip. Finally, I built up my muscles or something, because I hardly ever have trouble anymore. When all three of us learned to tack up without help, Carla took us out and bought us ice cream to celebrate.

At first, we would only ride the ponies at a walk around the ring until we learned to keep our heels down and our hands still and our eyes forward looking over the ponies' heads. There is a lot to remember. I especially had trouble keeping my eyes forward because I was always looking around to see what the others were doing and to see if I was doing everything right.

Carla always tells us, "Go forward and believe in it."

After all three of us had good positions at the walk, we learned to do two-point position so we could trot. It is sort of like halfway standing up and sitting down at the same time. Your legs hurt afterward because Carla explained you don't use those muscles much except for riding. The trot is a lot faster than the walk. It is scary and you think you will bounce off. After we learned two-point, we learned to post the trot. That is something like bouncing up and down, only you don't actually bounce if you're doing it right. If you do it wrong, you do bounce and it hurts your butt. We spent a lot of time learning to post. Carla spent a lot of time telling us to go forward and believe in it.

When I went to visit Aunt Hannah and told her about how hard it was, she said that there are some horses that don't trot. They do something called a rack or a running walk and you just sit on them and never worry about bouncing and it is like flying because it is so smooth. I think she might be kidding me because I've never seen a horse that doesn't bounce.

"How can a horse run and walk at the same time?" I asked her. She said she doesn't know, but she said that her father a long time ago used to raise that kind of horse and she can remember when the old barn was filled with horses.

"What happened to all the horses?" I wanted to know. "Where are they now?"

She said that people stopped buying horses because cars and tractors had taken over. Nobody wanted a horse anymore and people like her father stopped raising them because they couldn't make any money.

"But I want a horse!" I told her. "And I know some other girls who do, too."

She told me that not many people felt like I did. Then I said why don't we walk down to see the barn, and she thought that was a good idea. My dog Boo was with us and he started to run in little happy circles because the barn is one of his favorite places on the farm.

It is an old barn with lots of stalls. Grandpa stores hay for his cows in the hayloft and most of the stalls. It is a little scary because mice live in the barn. That's why Boo likes the barn so much. He likes to catch mice and crunch them. I think it is so gross. That's why I hadn't gone to the barn very much before. When we first got Boo two years ago, he ran right to the barn and crunched a mouse and it made me sick to see it. Also, Uncle Jack and Mommy thought there were too many places in the barn where I could get hurt because I might be tempted to jump out of the hayloft or something.

Before, I had never thought about how this barn was where horses lived just like the stable in Roanoke. I only thought about it as a place to keep the cow hay. But now, as Aunt Hannah and I walked into it, I noticed a sign on the first door that said. "Lady Luck."

"That was your last horse, wasn't it?" I asked Aunt Hannah.

"Yes," she said, "and she was a hunter, too—just like the kind of horses you take lessons on. Daddy made fun of me when I bought her—'We've not had a trotting horse on the place for over fifty years,' he said—but he liked her all the same. I used to gallop across these hills on her. She could fly."

Then she stopped talking and her eyes got a sad look in them. I didn't know what to say.

Then she said, "I vowed when Lady died that I'd never have my heart broken by losing another one. I'd had her over twenty-five years when she—."

"Died with her head in your arms," I whispered.

"Yes," said Aunt Hannah and she wiped her sleeve across her eyes. "Right in this very stall. She went down and never got up. I lay beside her and held her head in my arms for hours. She looked up at me just like she was saying good-by. Then—well, horses break your heart. They give you great joy, but in the end they always break your heart. You keep that in mind if you're so set on having a horse someday."

I didn't know what to say again. We just stood in the empty stall. I looked around. The stall had big gobs of spider webs hanging from the ceiling. Dust was all over the boards. It needed a good cleaning. A rusty bucket lay in one corner.

Then I said, "Maybe we could clean up her stall and make it look nice again."

"I guess we could do that," Aunt Hannah said. "Besides, maybe if you see how much work is involved in looking after a horse, you'll give up the notion of wanting one. You haven't cantered all around the ring yet, have you?"

"No," I told her. "I'm hardly able to trot all the way around yet. You're going to keep your promise, aren't you? You're going to get me a horse when I can canter the full circle?"

"Did I ever promise that?" she said. "I must have been crazy at the time. I don't remember ever making such a wild promise as that." Then she smiled, so I figured she was just playing with me.

We worked all morning and into the afternoon. We swept and dusted and raked. Once a mouse ran out from under the hay and I screamed, but Boo got him. This time I was glad that Boo was here.

When we finished cleaning the stall, we were so tired we could hardly move. But the stall looked ready for a horse to move right in.

"See," said Aunt Hannah. "I told you that horses were a lot of work. When I was your age, I used to help Daddy clean ten stalls each day. Sometimes I thought we'd never finish."

I told her that I wish I lived back then when the barn was full of horses, and she said that she wished she could go back to those days too. I thought for a long time about horses that don't trot and tried to imagine what one would look like and how Aunt Hannah looked when she was my age, but it is hard to think about things that you've never seen.

When Mommy came to get me, Aunt Hannah told her how hard I'd worked on cleaning the stall.

"I really wish you wouldn't encourage these fantasies," Mommy said.

"Anne-Lee," said Aunt Hannah, "I reckon you'd better face the fact that Joanna is a patch on the old family quilt."

Patches on the Same Quilt

What she said did not make a whole lot of sense to me. On the way home, I asked Mommy about it.

"It means," she said, "you're a chip off the old block."

That didn't make any sense either. Sometimes grown-ups can be very hard to understand.

Back in Roanoke, I'd think about the clean empty stall and wonder what kind of horse or pony would live in it. I thought about that stall a lot.

During my riding lesson, I really wanted to canter, but it seemed so scary. We started jumping over cross rails at the trot and sometimes the ponies would canter a little after they jumped, but I always got scared and pulled back on the reins.

Carla fussed at me more than once for doing it. "All you have to do is go forward and believe in it," she said to me.

I began to think I'd never learn to ride well enough to get my own horse. It just wasn't fair!

In May, I got to spend the whole weekend with Aunt Hannah because my parents were going on some kind of trip called a convention and children weren't allowed. That's what they said. I felt sad that I couldn't go, but they said Boo and I could stay with Aunt Hannah for the whole weekend, so that made everything all right. I even got to miss school on Friday, but Mommy said it is so close to the end of the year that I wouldn't miss anything important. They took me to Aunt Hannah's on Thursday night. It was nearly dark when we got there. As soon as we turned onto the dirt road, Boo started to bark—"Boof! Boof! Boof!"—like he always does. Aunt Hannah and Uncle Jack always know we're coming because they can hear Boo barking. That's what Aunt Hannah told me. It must be true because they're always standing on the porch when we get there.

"Did you hear Boo?" I always say.

"Boo who?" says Aunt Hannah.

"Well, you don't have to cry about it," I always say. It is our favorite joke.

Mommy and Daddy visited for awhile, and Boo ran to the barn to check for mice like he always does. Then Mommy and Daddy said it was still a long way to Richmond so they'd better go on, and then they left.

Aunt Hannah took me and Boo up the steps to the room where I always stayed and tucked me in under a thick, soft quilt. After she left, I lay awake for awhile and listened to the noises that the old house made. I used to be afraid at night, but I got over it. Besides, Boo was under the bed and would keep me safe. I tried to pretend that the house noises were the sounds of horses' hooves, but the sounds didn't match. Finally I fell asleep.

On Friday morning, Aunt Hannah and I walked over the farm and enjoyed the spring weather. She decided this would be a good day to clean off the graveyard up on the hill.

"Used to," she explained, "we'd clean off the graveyard every Decoration Day. That comes toward the end of this month. We'd pack a box lunch and spend the whole day fixing up the graveyard. Everybody'd do it. It was a tradition. I don't guess many folks do that anymore."

As we puffed and climbed the hill, I said, "It would be easier to get up here if we had a horse to ride."

Aunt Hannah agreed. "I reckon I've ridden a horse up here many a time," she said.

Finally we got to the top. I helped Aunt Hannah rake leaves and pull weeds, and she told me about the people who were up there. Her father was there, and his mother behind him, and his uncle that he was named for who died because of a war, and both his grandparents, and both his wives—one on either side. Beside one wife was a little tiny grave with a lamb on it. It was the only one without a name on it. Uncle Willie's grave had a fancy tombstone with a flag carved on it. He died a big hero in some war, too. There were some real old graves, too, so old you could hardly make out the writing on them. I should have been scared with all the dead people around me, but I wasn't. We worked all day, and I was so tired I could hardly eat supper.

The next day, Aunt Hannah said, "I've got a surprise for you. There's a horse show over in Gretna, and I thought maybe we could go. I haven't been to a horse show for a long time and I reckon it's time I went again."

"I've never been to a horse show," I told her. "I reckon it's time I went to one too."

Patches on the Same Quilt

We asked Uncle Jack to go with us, but he said he'd just as soon stay home and keep Boo company. "I'm not as crazy about horses as you two are," he said.

It seemed to take forever to get to Gretna, but Aunt Hannah said it was only twenty miles. The show was at an elementary school. As we drove into the school yard, a man took money from Aunt Hannah and gave us a program. I told Aunt Hannah I wish Huff Lane had horse shows in the schoolyard, but she said that this only happened once a year. They had put up a fence around the ball-field. If you looked hard, you could make out where the bases would be. I wondered what if a baseball game was scheduled on the same day as the horse show, but Aunt Hannah said she didn't reckon that happened. All over the school yard were trucks and horse trailers and horses. I'd never seen so many horses together in one place before. Some people rode their horses around the grounds. I guess they were practicing. Aunt Hannah quick yanked me out of the way before a tall thin horse with no mane and the top of its tail shaved off nearly ran me over.

"We'd better sit down," Aunt Hannah said. "Your mother would have a fit if you got trampled."

We took a seat in the bleachers. I looked through the program, but I couldn't figure out what some of the classes were supposed to be. Aunt Hannah put on her glasses and studied it.

The show finally started. Everybody stood up when they played "The Star-Spangled Banner" and a man on a horse cantered around the ring carrying the flag.

The first few classes had young horses that were just led in the ring. I think they were too young to ride. The judge looked them over and then they got ribbons. Then there were a bunch of classes where horses were ridden. Aunt Hannah and I decided to bet on who would win. I always tried to pick the prettiest horse, but that wasn't always the one who won.

You've got to watch how they move," said Aunt Hannah. "The best mover should place the highest. Also, you don't want a horse to break gait or take the wrong lead. Do you know what a lead is?" she asked me.

"Sort of," I said. "It's when they canter. But I don't know how to tell leads yet."

"You have to watch the legs. One side of a horse's body always leads the other. That means the legs on that side are always in front of the legs on the other side. When horses go around a circle, you want the legs on the inside to lead. That keeps the horse in better balance. Otherwise his legs might slip out from under him on the turns."

"Oh," I said. Aunt Hannah knew everything about horses.

We sat and watched a bunch more of classes, but I still liked to pick the prettiest horse. I started watching the legs more and more, though. Finally we got tired of sitting and decided to walk around the grounds to get a closer look at some of the horses. This time, Aunt Hannah kept me close to her. Every so often, we stopped to admire some of the horses tied to trailers, and a lot of people let me pet their horses when I said I liked horses.

A big truck pulling a big shiny silver trailer came in. The windows of the trailer were open, and you could see horses poking their heads out to look. Chains held their heads up high. I hoped someone would soon unchain the horses and let them out, so I could see them better. One of the horses had bright red hair—I think you call it chestnut—and a wide white blaze on its face.

"Look, Aunt Hannah!" I said. "Isn't that one beautiful?"

She agreed that it was. We went back to our seats and watched some more of the show. Later, we went back to the big trailer, but the horses were still chained up. The day was getting hot. I worried that they might be thirsty. I could hear the stomp of the pretty red horse's hooves as he kept shifting from side to side. His eyes looked wild. He must not be comfortable. I didn't see the driver of the truck anywhere around. I worried about the horse. He must be tired of standing there. If this was my horse, I'd treat him better. Aunt Hannah took my hand and led me away. Maybe she was thinking the same thing I was. We walked around and looked at other horses. We went to a hot-dog stand and got something to eat. We looked at saddles and bridles and all kinds of horse stuff that someone had for sale. We went back to the bleachers and watched some more of the show. When the day show was over, we went in the school cafeteria and ate supper. I told Aunt Hannah I'd like to see the pretty red horse when he showed. I bet he'd win. Aunt Hannah said she reckoned we could stay for a little of the night show—but only until we saw that horse.

After supper, we went back to the trailer. The horse was finally out. Something was the matter with his feet. They were huge! And he had chains around his legs! I'd never seen horse feet look like that.

"Aunt Hannah!" I said, "What's the matter with his feet? What's wrong with him?"

"He's a *she*," Aunt Hannah said. "Her feet have had pads nailed to them to jack her up and make her move different. Some people think horses look flashier that way."

"Well, I don't!" I said. "It's ugly. That's not the way horses should look!"

"I agree with you," Aunt Hannah said. "It is ugly. My daddy thought so, too. People were just starting to pad up show horses right before he died. He once told me, 'That's not how horses ought to go. There's nothing prettier than a horse moving out the way God intended—and nothing uglier than man trying to improve on nature.' I tend to agree with him."

"But the chains—?" I couldn't figure out the reason for them. "Why?"

"They bang on a horse's legs and make it step up higher," said Aunt Hannah. "Now, hush!"

We moved a little further away from the trailer but close enough so we could still watch. A foreign-looking dark-haired boy put a saddle and bridle on the horse and attached some pretty blue ribbons to the horse's mane. A pretty lady in a fancy riding suit with a number pinned to her back came out of a dressing room in the front of the trailer. A fat man without much hair walked up to her. I could hear a little of what they said, but it didn't make a lot of sense.

"Now you hold her in the first way of the ring," the fat man told the woman. "On the reverse, spur her hard on the outside and turn her loose." Then he said to the dark-haired boy, "José, is that mare ready for the DQP yet?"

"What's a DQP?" I asked Aunt Hannah.

"That's a government man who is supposed to inspect the horses to make sure—." She stopped for a minute and thought. "—to make sure they're all right."

I didn't exactly understand this. I decided to keep quiet and watch. The fat man ran his hands over the horse's legs. I could see him frown, but I couldn't make out what he said. Then he got a rag and dipped it in a bucket of water and washed off the horse's legs and dried them. Then the pretty lady mounted the horse and rode off while the dark-haired boy and fat man walked along. I wanted to follow, but Aunt Hannah said we'd better not. A few minutes later they came back. The pretty lady was walking and looked upset. The fat man looked like he was apologizing to her.

"What am I going to ride now?" she asked him. "I could have won this class!"

"Take my gelding," the fat man said. "He's good enough to go for two classes. He might not win, but you'll place high. I'll get one of the boys to saddle him."

"I want to win, not place!" the lady said. She ripped her number off her coat and threw it down. "You said I'd win! And now look! Maybe it's time I found another trainer!" She went into the dressing room and slammed the door.

The fat man went over to the dark-haired boy who was taking the saddle off the horse. He said a lot of bad words that I can't repeat. I thought he was going to hit the dark-haired boy.

"You stupid wet-back!" He yelled, "What were you trying to do—burn her leg up? I told you—only a few drops of diesel fuel in the pocket. Not up her whole leg! And you want to be a trainer. You can't even make it as groom!"

He said some more bad words while he told the boy he was fired. "This mare could have won the stake. Now she's worthless! You hear me? Worthless! Now what am I gonna do with her? Not that I could do anything with a year's suspension!" He said a lot more bad words—louder than before.

Aunt Hannah, who had been silent all during this, suddenly walked toward him and spoke up.

"I'll give you a thousand dollars for the mare," said Aunt Hannah. "I'll write you a check right now if you'll sign her papers over to me."

I couldn't believe what I was hearing. Aunt Hannah was buying a horse!

"She's worth five times that easy," said the fat man.

"I reckon she isn't," said Aunt Hannah. "Not now. Not at least for the next year. It costs plenty to keep a horse for a year—doesn't it? Especially a horse you can't show."

"Will you back date the check so you would've owned her before this show?" he asked. I don't know why that would matter.

"Sure," said Aunt Hannah, "on the condition that you'll deliver *my* horse to *my* home tonight. You're going right by my turn-off. I know the only way you can get back to Interstate 81 is to go west on Route 40 until you get to Route 220. I'm not far off Route 40."

My Aunt Hannah is one smart woman. The man agreed to do it. She wrote a check while he fumbled behind the truck's seat and found a packet of papers. He pulled one out and scribbled on it. He handed it to her at the exact same moment she handed him the check.

I really wanted to go and pet the horse—Aunt Hannah's horse!—but she held me back.

"Not now," she whispered. "There'll be plenty of time for that later. Lord, Jack will have a conniption fit."

The horse show went on even after it was dark. We sat and sat and watched and watched. Some people might get bored, but I didn't. I could never look at horses enough. Finally, we saw the fat man putting his horses back in the trailer. Aunt Hannah went over to him and told him where to turn off, that we'd be right behind him. Then she got her car and we got in and waited at the entrance until we saw his truck pull out. Aunt Hannah started up behind him and followed.

It was late when the truck pulled off the highway and onto the road that leads to Aunt Hannah's road. At the place where he was supposed to turn onto the dirt road to go to Aunt Hannah's, he stopped and got out of the truck. Aunt Hannah got out of the car.

"What's going on?" she said. "We had a deal."

"Look, lady," he said, "it's late. I brought the horse this far. I'm not gonna tear up my rig on that cow path you call a road. You're on your own now."

He motioned to one of the boys in the truck. "Unload that—." I can't say the words he used, but the boy opened the trailer door, unhooked the horse, led her off, and handed the rope to Aunt Hannah. Then, the man closed up the truck, everyone got back in, and they drove away. Aunt Hannah and the horse and I stood there in the road in the dark. None of us knew what to do.

"Well," said Aunt Hannah, "At least there's a full moon. If it were pitch dark, we'd really have problems. Now you can stay in the car and keep the doors locked until I get back, or you can walk with me. We still have a mile to go. It's up to you."

"I'll walk with you," I said. Even with the moon and all the stars, it still seemed pretty dark. Country dark is darker than city dark.

Aunt Hannah got her flashlight from the glove compartment. That helped a little. The three of us started out. The horse walked slowly, and her big clunky shoes weren't meant for country roads in the middle of the night. We found the turn-off into the driveway and went past my grand-parents' trailer. I wanted to knock on the door and wake them up and show them what we had, but Aunt Hannah shushed me.

"No use to worry them," she said.

Finally, we got to the house. Aunt Hannah yelled, and Uncle Jack turned on the outside lights and came out. Boo came out barking, but he stopped in his tracks when he saw the horse. He hid behind Uncle Jack and peeped around.

"Oh, Hannah," Uncle Jack said, "Tell me this is a bad dream and you're not really standing there with a horse."

"OK," said Aunt Hannah, "You're dreaming. It's night and I'm standing here with a mare. I guess that makes it a nightmare."

"Not funny," said Uncle Jack. "You do have a reasonable explanation for this, don't you?"

"Yes," said Aunt Hannah, "but I haven't thought of it yet. Now, if you'll be so kind, please grab a lantern and light the way to the barn for us."

He did. We got the horse in the stall and I found a bucket and filled it with water for her. Uncle Jack carried it into the stall. The horse drank and drank. Uncle Jack refilled the bucket. Aunt Hannah got some of the cow hay and opened a bale in the stall. While the horse ate, Uncle Jack drove us back to get Aunt Hannah's car. Neither of them said much the whole way, and I was too sleepy to be much of a talker. I snuggled up on the back seat with Boo and I think I went to sleep.

Aunt Hannah must have put me to bed, because when I woke up the next morning, I didn't remember going to bed and my teeth felt funny like they hadn't been brushed. At first, right after I woke up, I thought I'd had a strange dream about going to a horse show and coming home with a horse. Then I remembered—it was real! Before I got out of bed, I could hear Aunt Hannah talking on the phone to someone.

"I know you don't do business on Sundays, Ed, but I really need a load of sawdust," she said. " And helping one of God's creatures counts a lot more, as far as I'm concerned, than sitting in a building listening to announcements about how the church needs money for a new roof. If you feel guilty about doing business on Sunday, then don't charge me for the sawdust and it won't be business. It'll fall into the category of loving thy neighbor."

I got up, got dressed, and went down to breakfast. I had no sooner finished eating when I heard Boo barking. The neighbor man was there already with a truck full of sawdust. While I closed Boo on the back porch, Aunt Hannah and Uncle Jack showed him where to take it. When I got to the barn, Aunt Hannah had already led the horse out of the stall while her neighbor dumped in the sawdust.

"Daggone!" said the neighbor. "I never seen such big clunky feet on a horse! How can a horse move dragging around feet like that?"

"Not very well," said Aunt Hannah, "and if you gentlemen will hold her for me, I'll see what I can do to get these shoes off her."

She went into what used to be the tack room and came back with a tool box like I'd seen the horseshoer at the stable use. She rooted around in the box and pulled out some funny-looking tools. While Uncle Jack held up the horse's leg and the neighbor held her head, Aunt Hannah cut the metal bands that held the shoe on. Then she pried up the nails. Finally she pulled off what she called pads and the shoe itself. It was so heavy I could hardly lift it. Then she did the other foot. When she was finished, the horse that looked so big before now didn't look nearly as big. I'll bet she was glad to get those awful things off her feet.

"Her legs are hot as fire, and swollen to boot" Said Aunt Hannah. "Maybe we should take her out and run the hose over them."

The horse limped out into the barn lot like she wasn't used to walking like a regular horse. I was worried that maybe she was ruined and would never walk right. Aunt Hannah let me hold the hose while the water ran on the horse's legs. The neighbor left while we were doing this. Before he left, he asked what the horse's name was. Aunt Hannah realized that she didn't know and sent Uncle Jack to the car to get the papers. He opened up the folded paper, looked at it, and started to laugh.

"Well, this is appropriate," he said. "Foolish Folly! She certainly is, Hannah. Buying this horse was pure folly—and foolish to boot."

"Let me see those papers," Aunt Hannah said. She let go of the horse, but the horse didn't go anywhere. "Foolish Folly, out of Folly's Fool," she read.

She laughed and let her fingers trace the list of names across the page. Suddenly she stopped laughing. Her finger pointed to a name close to the edge. "Joyful Air," she said, "by Jubilation. That was Daddy's breeding stallion. Oh, my lord—she's one of ours!"

For a moment, I thought Aunt Hannah was going to cry. She went on. "I was a lot younger than you are now when Daddy went down to Tennessee in 1935. He told me that he met with a whole bunch of men to work on getting a registry started—that was so they could keep track of the horses' bloodlines, you know. A lot of the horses like he raised were in Tennessee, and he did a lot of selling and trading down there. I always wanted to go, but my brother Willie was the one he'd take. I wanted so bad to be part of it, but I was too little, he said, and Willie was such a good rider...." Her voice dropped off. "By the time I could have gone, I'd already moved to Richmond with Doreen. What with the war and Willie getting killed and all, Daddy sort of gave up traveling to shows and sales and such. By the time I came back home, Daddy had sold off most of the breeding stock. He kept a few horses for his own use—he rode right up until he was eighty and then drove a buggy for a few years after that—but it was never again the way it once was. I'm glad Daddy isn't here to see what's become of the beautiful horses he bred. He always took pride in naturally gaited, free-moving horses—not like this. He always said it was useless for man to try to improve on what God intended."

Again, I thought she might cry.

"Well," she said, "We can't save them all, but we can save this one. I might be a foolish old lady, but I can save this one."

"What are you going to do with her, Hannah?" asked Uncle Jack. "Surely, you're not going to start riding again at your age."

"And why not?" said Aunt Hannah. "I'm barely sixty-one. I've got twenty good riding years left—and then I'll slow down and start driving."

"No use for me to try to reason with you, is there?" said Uncle Jack.

"Nope," she said, "This is my folly and I intend to enjoy it." She winked at me.

Aunt Hannah found some old brushes and we started brushing Folly. Seemed like she enjoyed it. One time she nuzzled my hair. It wasn't long until my parents drove in. I guess they couldn't find anyone at the house and decided to walk down to the barn. Mommy took one look at Folly and me and thought that Folly was my horse.

"Oh, Aunt Hannah," she said, "You didn't!? Joanna doesn't need a horse right now! She's too young—!"

"Whoa!" said Aunt Hannah. "Who said anything about this mare being Joanna's? As a matter of fact, she's mine!"

We put Folly back in her stall and walked back to the house. While I got my things together, I could hear Aunt Hannah explaining everything to Mommy and Daddy.

On Monday, at my riding lesson. I cantered about ten strides before I lost my nerve. For the first time, I noticed that the horses and ponies that I had once thought were so beautiful now looked plain and ordinary. Not one could compare to Folly. By Tuesday, I was begging to spend the following weekend at Aunt Hannah's. Since the weather was getting warm enough for Mommy to sit on the porch at the condo and look at the lake and get ideas, she said it would be O.K. The rest of the week seemed to crawl by.

Early Saturday morning, when Mommy let us out of the car, Boo and I ran all the way to the barn without stopping. Aunt Hannah was already there. She was finishing the fence where there used to be a small paddock so Folly could go in it. Aunt Hannah explained that you didn't want to turn a horse out that wasn't used to grass. It could kill them. I didn't know that. I thought all horses liked grass. You have to introduce them to it gradually, she said, so they get used to it. She told me she'd been hand-walking Folly a little more each day.

"Let me just get the gate onto its hinges," she said, "and we'll turn her out and see how she likes it. You better lock Boo up in one of the stalls so he doesn't excite her."

I did what she said. I put Boo in a stall that had some old bales in it and he started looking for mice. Aunt Hannah dragged the gate to the opening in the fence and wrestled it onto the hinges. I helped her by holding up the bottom so it wouldn't slip out of place. It was heavy. Finally we got it hung. Then Aunt Hannah went into the barn. I followed her. Folly nickered when she saw us.

"You want to go out, don't you?" said Aunt Hannah as she slipped a halter over Folly's head and fastened the buckles.

Patches on the Same Quilt

You'd better stand out of the way," she said to me. "Likely Folly'll be a bit frisky."

She wasn't, though. She walked out like a perfect lady. When Folly was in the paddock, Aunt Hannah undid the halter and turned her loose. Folly stood for a moment, then snorted. She looked around, and pawed at the ground with a front hoof. Then she put her head down and sniffed the ground. Carefully, she tasted a blade of grass, then another and another. Then she put up her head and sniffed the air as if she was tasting freedom for the first time in her life. She put her head down and kicked out her back heels. Then she ran. She ran and ran around the paddock, sometimes neighing at us as if she wanted us to run with her. Of course we couldn't. From inside the barn, Boo barked to answer her neighs. Aunt Hannah and I sat on the edge of the fence and watched her. She was the most beautiful horse I'd ever seen in my life.

Suddenly, Folly stopped running and came over to Aunt Hannah and put her head on Aunt Hannah's shoulders. Aunt Hannah reached up and scritch-scritched Folly's ears.

"I reckon," said Aunt Hannah, "that I just might try to ride this mare. You'll pick me up if I get thrown, won't you, Joanna?"

I didn't know if she was kidding or not. She went into the tack room and came out with an old saddle and bridle which looked like they'd just been cleaned and oiled. I guess maybe Aunt Hannah had been planning to ride all along. She called Folly to her, put the halter back on, and hitched her to a metal ring that was attached on the side of the barn. She carefully put the saddle on and tightened the girth. Folly didn't budge. Then she slipped the halter around Folly's neck and put the bridle over her head. Folly opened her mouth and took the bit.

"So far, so good," said Aunt Hannah. She undid the halter and led Folly to a stump and patted her neck. Then she climbed on the stump, put her foot in the stirrup, and swung herself up like she might have been a young girl and not an old lady at all. Folly never budged until Aunt Hannah said, "Come up, Folly," and tightened her leg just a tiny bit. Folly moved out at a fast walk. Aunt Hannah rode her up and down the driveway a few times. Folly never once acted up.

"Well," said Aunt Hannah, "Let's see what Folly can really do."

She tightened her leg a little more and Folly moved off like she was flying. She wasn't cantering and she wasn't trotting. It looked like she was running and walking both at the same time. I watched Aunt Hannah's shoulders to see if they bounced up and down like they do at a trot. Aunt Hannah was perfectly still. There was a big smile on her face.

She rode up beside me.

"Do you want to see if Folly will double? Want to chance it? We might get dumped."

"Yes!" I said.

So what if I got dumped! I wanted to ride this beautiful mare. I climbed up on the stump and Aunt Hannah sort of dragged me up behind her. It was higher than I thought it would be. I wound my arms around Aunt Hannah's waist and decided to hang on for dear life. If I fell off, I figured, Mommy'd probably never let me come back.

Aunt Hannah clucked to Folly and we started off. We were moving fast, then faster. I kept waiting to bounce, but I never did. I never knew riding could be like this. I could do this all day. Then Aunt Hannah turned off the driveway and headed for the big pasture.

"There's nothing to compare to riding a fine horse across your own land," Aunt Hannah said. "That's what Daddy always told me."

She clucked to Folly again, and all of a sudden we were cantering. Folly had big loose strides, not choppy like Tidbit's. At first I was afraid, but then my body started to move in Folly's rhythm, sort of like being on a rocking horse when you're a little bitty kid, and I decided that this was nothing to be afraid of. It was great! We circled the whole pasture before Aunt Hannah brought Folly down to a walk. She dropped the reins loose so Folly could stretch and relax. Folly headed back to the barn. She knew where her home was.

Patches on the Same Quilt

"You always walk your horse loose at the beginning and end of a ride," Aunt Hannah said. "That way the horse'll last a long time."

"I know," I told her. "That's what my riding teacher always says."

"We'd better get Folly back to the barn and get her cleaned up," Aunt Hannah said. "The vet is coming to see her today."

I feared the worst. There must be something wrong with Folly—something terrible that Aunt Hannah didn't want to tell me.

"Is she sick?" I asked.

"No, I don't think so," Aunt Hannah replied. "But I don't have any record of her immunizations and the Coggins test that was with her papers has almost expired. Plus, it's a good idea to have a new horse vetted, just to make sure everything is all right."

By the time the vet pulled his truck up beside the barn, we'd put Folly back in her stall and had curried and brushed her so much that she gleamed.

"Fine looking horse," he said to Aunt Hannah. "Now what is it you want me to do?"

"Well, Doc" said Aunt Hannah, "I have no way of knowing if her shots are up-to-date, so you'd better immunize her for everything. Her Coggins is about to expire, so you'd better pull some blood for a test. I think she was treated pretty rough, so you'd better go over her thoroughly, just in case."

"Will do," said the vet. He smiled. "You're not thinking about showing her, are you Hannah? I mean, at your age—"

"There's no telling what I might decide to do," said Aunt Hannah, "but I want to be ready, just in case."

I really wanted to stay and watch, but Aunt Hannah told me to wait outside the barn while the vet did whatever he had to do to Folly. I hoped it wouldn't hurt. I got Boo out and we went for a walk along the creek so he could look in groundhog holes.

We got back about the time the vet finished.

"Well, Doc," said Aunt Hannah, "What's the verdict?"

"You have a fine horse, there's no doubt about that," he said, "but I'm a little worried about the tendon on her right fore.

You'd better not ride her too hard for a while. Of course, before long, you won't be riding her at all, so I guess that leg will heal up fine."

Why wouldn't we ride her? What could be the matter? My mind ran wild.

"Why not?" said Aunt Hannah. "If you're going to start up again about me being too old to ride—"

The vet smiled. "Your mare is between five and six months pregnant," he said. "You'll want to stop riding her in a month or two. A little light riding until then won't hurt her—might even get her in better shape. Just don't over-stress that leg."

Pregnant! That meant—a baby! Folly was going to have a baby! I couldn't believe what I was hearing!

"You wouldn't kid me, Doc?" said Aunt Hannah. "The previous owner never said a thing—"

"He's not the most respectable person to deal with," said the vet. "Likely he didn't want to give you the satisfaction of getting the foal's papers. You won't be able to register the foal, you know. That lets out showing it in any big shows."

"You can't ride papers," said Aunt Hannah, but I could tell she was a little disappointed.

After the vet had gone, I asked Aunt Hannah the question I was dying to ask.

"Will the baby be mine?" I said. "Will that be the horse you'll get for me?"

"The foal isn't here yet," Aunt Hannah said, "and when it gets here, it won't be rideable for a few years. Are you sure you can wait that long?"

"Maybe you could lend me Folly while I wait," I said.

"Maybe," she said. "Maybe I could do that. We'll see. Besides, you still haven't cantered all the way around the ring, have you?"

She knew I hadn't.

When Mommy came to get me, I told her the big news. She rolled her eyes and didn't say much. On the way home, I thought about all the things that had happened in the last few weeks.

"I want to live on the farm someday," I said to Mommy.

"Well," she said, "one day, it will likely be yours. Neither your Uncle J.D. nor your Aunt Sarah wants to come back to it. Grandpa will probably leave you his half, and I'm pretty sure Aunt Hannah is going to will you hers. What would you do with the farm?"

"I'll raise horses," I said, "beautiful horses that don't bounce when you ride them fast. And I'll write books about them so everybody would know what they're like. And maybe I'll draw pictures of them and put the pictures in the books."

"Sounds like you'll be busy," Mommy said.

"I reckon I will," I said.

Boo snuggled up beside me on the seat. I rode the rest of the way home in silence and thought about all the horses I'd have when I was grown. I didn't care if they'd break my heart. I thought about Folly's foal that would be running around by this time next year. I tried to think of a good name for it.

Well, that was last weekend. Today at my riding lesson, when it came time to canter, I gave the cue just the way I was supposed to—raise the inside rein, squeeze at the girth with my inside leg, put my outside leg behind the girth and use it to bump the pony a little bit. The pony went into the correct lead. I remembered to keep my position. I kept my eyes in the direction I was going and didn't look around.

I went forward and I believed in it.

Suddenly, it seemed so easy—there was nothing to it. I cantered all the way around the ring without stopping.

I went the full circle.

The End